The item should be returned or renewed by the last date stamped below.

Dylid dychwelyd neu adnewyddu'r eitem erbyn y dyddiad olaf sydd wedi'i stampio isod

Newport
CITY COUNCIL
CYNGOR DINAS
Casnewydd

WFS

To renew visit / Adnewyddwch ar
www.newport.gov.uk/libraries

BUTCHER'S WOOD

Also by Peter Guttridge

The Brighton mystery series

CITY OF DREADFUL NIGHT *
THE LAST KING OF BRIGHTON *
THE THING ITSELF *
THE DEVIL'S MOON *
THOSE WHO FEEL NOTHING *
SWIMMING WITH THE DEAD *
THE LADY OF THE LAKE *

The Nick Madrid series

NO LAUGHING MATTER
A GHOST OF A CHANCE
TWO TO TANGO
THE ONCE AND FUTURE CON
FOILED AGAIN
CAST ADRIFT

* available from Severn House

BUTCHER'S WOOD

Peter Guttridge

SEVERN
HOUSE

First world edition published in Great Britain and the USA in 2021
by Severn House, an imprint of Canongate Books Ltd,
14 High Street, Edinburgh EH1 1TE.

Trade paperback edition first published in Great Britain and the USA in 2022
by Severn House, an imprint of Canongate Books Ltd.

severnhouse.com

British Library Cataloguing-in-Publication Data
A CIP catalogue record for this title is available from the British Library.

ISBN-13: 978-0-7278-5037-9 (cased)
ISBN-13: 978-1-78029-788-0 (trade paper)
ISBN-13: 978-1-4483-0527-8 (e-book)

All Severn House titles are printed on acid-free paper.

Typeset by Palimpsest Book Production Ltd.,
Falkirk, Stirlingshire, Scotland.
Printed and bound in Great Britain by
TJ Books, Padstow, Cornwall.

*For my late great friends: Barnaby Hall,
photographer extraordinaire; John Benfield, an actor's actor;
Czeslaw Doniewski, artist, sculptor and designer.*

The privileges of beauty are enormous.

Jean Cocteau

*Love seemed to be holding my heart in his hand and my
lady in his arms, sleeping. Then he awakened her and that
burning heart he made her, fearful, eat*

Dante Alighieri – 'To Every Captive Soul
and Gentle Heart'

PROLOGUE

Nimue Grace, former Hollywood actress, read the name on the sign with something of a shiver. Butcher's Wood. She'd been in enough rubbishy thrillers to imagine why it might be called that. Some psycho butchering his victims there. More likely, of course, it was . . . well, what? What on earth would an actual butcher be doing working in a wood? The sign didn't explain why it had such a grisly-sounding name, just that it was an ancient woodland administered by the Woodland Trust.

Still, at least it wasn't midnight and down some lonely alley or, worse, in a graveyard. God, she hated that kind of lazy plotting in movies. Then again, a wood wasn't much better – the girl running away and inevitably tripping over a tree root, so the madman could pounce.

She started walking along the narrow path before she scared herself out of it. She'd come back on the train from a rare trip to London and got off at Hassocks to go and see an elderly old friend, an ex-neighbour. Her friend lived about a mile from the station in one of the apartments in Danny House, an Elizabethan mansion that had been partly converted into apartments for the elderly. She'd decided to walk there across the fields, which had led her to this wood.

It was beautiful here; all ancient oak and hazel. Hawthorn too, which her parents always referred to by one of its old names: Queen of May. There were vibrant bluebells as far as she could see. And carpets of wild garlic, their white flowers also vibrant.

She loved woods. In some Welsh legends, Nimue was a wood nymph, though more usually the name was linked to water. And in some versions of the Arthurian legends she was the Lady of the Lake. Nimue Grace actually did have her own lake, in the middle of her own wood, over in Plumpton.

Occasionally, she camped there. Of course, it was much more

fun doing it with someone else but she was happy to be independent and single. She didn't pine for a relationship just for the sake of it. And she was wary of men. The twice she'd really given her heart – and soul, why not use the cliché? – the consequences had been devastating. Both times she had been far too trusting and had chosen the wrong men.

She was aware that, as Jean Cocteau had famously said, the privileges of beauty were enormous. She had certainly benefited from those privileges – she wasn't going to deny that she had been blessed with beauty – but she had tried to be respectful of that in her dealings with other people.

However, the other side of that coin was that her beauty made her a target for unscrupulous people. Beauty combined with an open heart had made her especially vulnerable. And she had paid the price, both emotionally and financially, for falling for their lies.

She saw a rough-looking, scrubby-bearded man in a shabby brown overcoat stumbling down the path towards her. *Oh God, here we go*, she thought, *lurching into slasher movie territory.*

He was looking at his feet, so she didn't think he'd seen her. She stepped off the path and walked diagonally through the bluebells away from him, intending to re-join the path near its exit from the wood.

That's how she came across it.

She saw the pretty red spots on the bluebells and wild garlic flowers first. Then she saw some were rust-coloured and wondered if the spots might be blood. Then she saw a bloodied and battered human body, its chest cavity gaping.

Staring at it horribly transfixed, swallowing rapidly, she recognized that, now at least, the name Butcher's Wood was entirely apt. She hoped a director would call 'Cut' and the corpse sit up, pull a packet of fags out of the chest cavity and light up. But nothing changed.

Then she remembered the rough-looking man. She looked round carefully, as if moving her head too quickly would alert him to her. Which maybe it would. She crouched behind a bush. She crouched and she waited.

Of course, all this came later . . .

ONE

T he first death occurred at the start of the second act. The actor playing Vincent, the young male lead, sat on the stage just in front of the white curtain that had been made to look like distressed wallpaper. It wasn't quite that he ignored the audience, more that he was in his own world. His long bare feet looked unusually white and almost prehensile in the shallow water he was dipping them in.

The white curtain began to bloom red behind his head. The audience thought it was part of the show – there was very little that would surprise them after the eccentricities of the first act. Anything was possible.

The actor playing Vincent turned to get back onstage and start the second act. He looked blankly at the red stain spreading rapidly across the curtain. He reached out a finger to touch it and recoiled, not so much at his finger coming away red as at the human face suddenly outlined like a death mask, nose and forehead prominent, as the reddened curtain adhered to it.

There was a sharp intake of breath from the audience and a couple of shrieks at this striking sight but, still, most of the people seemed to think it was part of the production. The actor playing Vincent looked more closely at his red finger then again at the face pressed against the curtain.

He gave an odd kind of shudder and fell backwards into the water, hitting the back of his head on the thick edge of the orchestra pit with both a hollow ring and a horrible squelching sound. And now at least some of those in the front row realized that this wasn't acting. Probably. That was when the screaming started.

His was the second death.

It had come as something of a relief to Detective Inspector Sarah Gilchrist when the screaming in the theatre started. She'd been silently screaming herself through the never-ending first act of the play. The production, she thought, was a load of pretentious twaddle. The young performers were just as irritating, especially one young actress, Elvira Somebody-or-Other. Gilchrist had quite liked her in something or other on the telly. Live she was so self-regarding and, well, *actressy*, that Gilchrist wished she had brought her Taser and had a seat nearer the stage.

It didn't help her irritation that there was hardly any leg room in the stalls, so she had been uncomfortable from the moment she sat down.

Then there was the fact that she wasn't a theatre-goer. She couldn't remember the last time she'd been here to see a play. In fact, the only performance she could remember seeing here was a Ken Dodd show, on a Sunday evening years ago when she had first been posted to Brighton. He went on for so long, the show seemed to end sometime the following Thursday. But at least he was entertaining. The first act of this play had bored her rigid.

She was in the audience at the invitation of her colleague, Sussex's chief pathologist, Frank Bilson. She assumed he'd be hating it too and have the same problem with the leg room as he was pretty lanky. Yet whenever she glanced at him, he seemed perfectly relaxed and actually absorbed in the play. She didn't look at him too often because he always seemed to sense it and would give her a look that indicated he might be misinterpreting her intent.

'This isn't a date,' Gilchrist had said for the umpteenth time as they were sipping their drinks on the balcony of the theatre while they were waiting for the play to begin. They were looking across the Pavilion Gardens at the sun giving the onion domes of the Royal Pavilion a golden aura. 'This is just two colleagues enjoying an evening at the theatre.'

'Sure, Sarah, I get it,' Bilson had said. 'But you will let me know when you've got bored with ostrich omelettes?'

Gilchrist had pursed her lips at that. The ostrich farmer in Plumpton she'd been seeing was very sweet.

Bilson had then leaned back against the rails and asked her what she knew about the play. At her shrug, he explained that it was a rarely performed 1950s play called *The Dinner Game* by a forgotten American playwright. According to Bilson, 'It leans heavily on Tennessee Williams *and* Arthur Miller which is quite a feat.' Gilchrist wouldn't know. It had a cast of four – a crippled daughter, a gay son, and a rugged longshoreman who was also a wannabe poet who was having a relationship with both of them and who their mother, played by the fourth member of the cast, fancied something rotten.

'So a bit like Pasolini's *Theorem* too,' Bilson had said, which totally passed Gilchrist by. This getting a cultural education lark kept revealing huge chasms of her ignorance – or other people's nerdiness.

Anyway, everyone was meant to be Italian but, again according to Bilson, colour-blind casting was the new orthodoxy in theatre and TV. So Giuseppe, the rugged longshoreman from Sicily, was played by an Afro-Caribbean actor with shoulder-length dreadlocks called Bob Thomas, last seen playing an East End drug dealer in some TV cop thing or other.

In her ignorance, Gilchrist expected there to be line changes to reflect the changed ethnicity of the longshoreman but no, Bilson said, the new theatre orthodoxy was not only blind but deaf. So Bob's character talked about growing up in the slums of Naples and his mamma's *pasta e fagioli* making him what he was and, *mamma mia*, how he missed Italy and he would go back there someday a success. All this delivered with a lovely Caribbean lilt, *mon*.

Bilson looked at Gilchrist now as he sat on the low wall of the orchestra pit. 'Broken neck and brain trauma, at first sight,' he said. He looked up at the face pressing into the curtain. 'It's what's going on behind there that interests me.'

'Me too, Frank,' she said, wading a couple of yards through the shallow water and hauling herself up onto the stage. She squelched as she walked to one wing. So much for dressing up for the theatre, she thought ruefully. She'd already phoned her sidekick, DS Bellamy Heap, and the incident unit at police HQ, but she was most certainly first on the scene.

And what a scene, she thought, as she saw the dead body leaning oddly against the curtain, with not much of the back of its head left, and blood covering the entire length of the back and pooling on the floor. Beside the body, a blood-stained lead weight lay tangled in a long rope. Gilchrist approached, warily looking up into the rafters from where the weight had presumably come.

There were a handful of people around the perimeter of the stage in various postures of distress and disgusted fascination. Gilchrist identified herself to them and asked them to gather together at the back of the stage. She stepped gingerly around the body. It was the self-regarding actress who had been giving such a terrible performance. Elvira Wright. The stage manager had confirmed it as Gilchrist had approached the stage.

She was crumpled over the Zimmer frame that seemed to have been central to her performance, her head with the massive head trauma pressing on the white curtain, her blood spreading across it. Gilchrist shunted away a naughty thought. She needn't have bothered.

'Everybody's a critic, eh, Sarah?' Bilson said as he came up beside her.

There had been a stampede of people leaving the theatre once the first screams started. Gilchrist understood that everybody was conditioned to think *terrorist attack* and stampede like a herd of gazelles at sight of a lion or a leopard or a tiger or whatever-the-hell predator gazelles attracted. Gilchrist wasn't up on her wildlife, just as she wasn't up on so much else.

She'd been the main sporty one at her school and hadn't been much interested in any other subject – unless a good-looking boy was in the class, of course. That was one of the reasons she'd been here tonight with Bilson. Trying to get a bit of culture to broaden her knowledge base.

The stampede followed a predictable course. People trampling over each other to preserve themselves. Gilchrist hated the myth that was so pervasive in the UK – and maybe in the rest of the world? – that people acted heroically in such situations. In her experience, a handful did but the rest were entirely selfish.

Actress Nimue Vivian Grace sat beneath her California pine – the nearest she got to Hollywood these days – in her South

Downs garden and plotted her next move. Not on the chess board in front of her. She almost knew this Fischer versus Spassky game she was playing by heart. She smiled. If only life could be as straightforward as a game of chess between two geniuses. Ha! But it wasn't and that was her dilemma.

She was going broke trying to hang on to her little piece of paradise in the Sussex countryside. She had turned her back on Hollywood and returned to her country of birth, licking her wounds from a woefully ill-judged and devastating relationship with a man who turned out to be a psychopath. In consequence, her income had plummeted. West End theatre just didn't cut it financially once she'd paid her agent, her VAT bill and her tax. She couldn't quite bring herself to do telly. Besides, her agent had warned her that if she did, it would damage her *brand*, but that advice seemed a bit out of date now.

In the meantime, she was sitting on a pile of money in old currency in her apple cellar. She was hoping to hear soon whether this money, stolen during the infamous Hassocks Blockade of the 1990s, was traceable before she took the lot to the Bank of England for conversion into modern currency. Until then she was stymied. If she couldn't find that out, then she couldn't take the risk of trying to get the money converted.

The money was a windfall. Not that she had stolen it. It had been found stashed in containers in her lake. *She* wasn't a bad person. She didn't think she had done anything *really* wrong by not declaring this money discovered there by the film student who had brought it to her. The banks it had been stolen from so many years before were covered by insurance. Nobody got hurt in the robbery. It was just her good fortune that the robbers dumped the money on her property before being punted off to jail for other crimes.

She did have some concerns that one of the robbers, Graham Goody, was incarcerated down the road in Lewes prison and he knew that at least some of the money had been found. But he wasn't due out for another five years, according to Bob Watts, the police commissioner who was Goody's old acquaintance and her new one.

Bob Watts had won her in a charity raffle – well, morning coffee with her – and then had been helpful when things were going murderously awry all around her. Grace intended to keep him close. Not at all so that she would know what was going on with regard to the money but because she thought it was time she should try to have some kind of relationship with a decent man. Her choice of men for most of her life in Hollywood and in the theatre had been dismal.

She knew that Watts and his friend Jimmy Tingley were going to Canada to rescue Bob's ex-wife from who-knew-what dodgy dealings that the ex-wife's second husband was involved in.

Good men. Men of integrity. Where had such men been all her life? Well, they'd been there, but they had looked boring and square to her self-loathing, take-advantage-of-me-bad-boy eyes.

Two hot-air balloons like inverted tears broke free of the line of trees and drifted into the air. They were far enough away that she couldn't see the sponsorship logos, just the gaudy colours. She heard the post van arrive on her drive on the other side of the high Victorian wall. She looked once more at the chessboard – she was being trounced by Spassky – then walked up the garden to her house. Only one letter lay on the doormat. It was postmarked Lewes. The handwriting was neat.

She picked up the Edwardian ivory letter opener she kept on the windowsill by her front door and slit the top of the envelope. Inside was a single sheet of paper neatly folded. She read it twice. *Dear Miss Grace, I'm pretty confident you have my money. I want it back. We need to talk before things get complicated for you.* It was signed *Graham Goody c/o Lewes Nick.*

TWO

When DS Bellamy Heap hurried into the theatre, he was accompanied by SOCO, who went ahead of him onto the stage. Gilchrist could hear ambulance sirens outside.

'You were on the scene very quickly,' Heap said. He glanced at Bilson examining the actress. 'Mr Bilson too.'

'It wasn't a date,' Gilchrist said. Heap looked puzzled and she flushed. 'We were colleagues at the theatre, that's all.'

Heap nodded and flushed too. 'Good play?'

'Lost play apparently. Lost production for me, but what do I know?'

'This is one of the actresses?' Heap said. Gilchrist nodded.

Bilson walked over to join them. 'Well, Sarah, it's pretty obvious she's dead from blunt trauma to the back and top of her skull. Inflicted by that lead weight beside her, dripping with blood. Sorry to be so Grand Guignol, but the theatre, you know . . .'

'What's that weight even doing here?' Gilchrist said.

'They use lead weights to raise and lower the fire curtain which comes down between acts. They operate on a pulley system.' He pointed up. 'In the old days, they'd be operated manually by a stagehand – lots of old sailors used to work backstage because up there it looks like the rigging of a ship – ropes and pulleys and curtains like sails and cross-bars for adding more curtains. This is a Frank Matcham theatre, so for its day it was technically very advanced.'

'You're losing me, as usual. I haven't even bothered to ask you about the Grand Whatsit. But you're saying we're dealing with two accidents, then?'

'The actor playing Vincent certainly was an accident. This one, Elvira Wright, I would have to wait until SOCO went up there' – he pointed into the rafters – 'and checked how that weight came down.' He gestured across to the group of people clustered at the back of the stage. 'What do they have to say?'

'Don't know yet,' Gilchrist said.

'Well, chop-chop I would say, Sarah. Chop-chop.'

Gilchrist and Heap looked back at the half-dozen people gathered at the back of the stage, giving statements to a couple of constables she didn't recognize. Heap led the way backstage to a sign for dressing rooms. There were names on all the doors. They knocked on the one for Bob Thomas.

'I didn't see nothing, woman,' Bob Thomas said. 'Elvira and Vincent have that first scene of the second act together. I was keeping Miss Grahame company in her dressing room.'

'Not *woman,* if you don't mind, Mr Thomas,' Gilchrist said. 'Detective Inspector Gilchrist will do nicely. So she was standing where she was meant to stand when she was killed?'

'Every night for the past month. I suppose that accidents happen, *Detective Inspector.*'

'Would you happen to know if Miss Grahame is still in her dressing room?'

'Went back to the Grand, I believe, when she heard the show was cancelled. That lady likes a cocktail or two.'

Nimue Grace's landline rang when she was just going out of the door. She hurried back and picked it up in the kitchen.

'Graham Goody here.'

'Who?'

'Ms Grace, give me enough respect not to pretend you don't know who I am and I'll be respectful enough not to mention how sexy you are.'

Grace took the phone out into the garden.

'How did you get my number?'

'Ways and means, Ms Grace.'

'What do you want?'

'As I said in my letter, I want my money.'

'Look, this is not a convenient time to talk. I have a taxi waiting outside to take me to the theatre and I'm already late.'

'This will only take a minute. You have my money and I want it.'

'Why on earth do you think I owe you money? I don't even know you.'

'Sure you do. And I didn't say you owe me money, I said you have my money. You know that. And I want it back.'

'Well, I'm aware of the Hassocks robbery that you're implicated in but never convicted of. Are you referring to that money? If so, I'd think you'd be wary of telling a stranger on an open phone line, from a prison no less, that you were involved in the robbery. I don't think there's a statute of limitations on that sort of thing is there?'

'Very slippery, Ms Grace. But this call can't be traced.'

'It can be recorded though,' she said with a calm she didn't feel.

There was a silence. 'You're recording this? Now why would you be doing that?'

'All my calls are automatically recorded. You can't believe the nutters who get hold of this number.' Actually, Grace had been advised to set up the recording system by the lawyer who was trying to help her when the creep George Bosanquet was terrorizing her. She had kept it in place just in case.

'Oh, I can, Ms Grace. The privileges of beauty have a downside.'

Grace gave a little start. 'You know Cocteau?'

'Some. There's not a lot of intellectual stimulation to be had in the nick, so anybody with a brain and curiosity – and I like to think I have both – turns to books. Or their Kindle, these days, of course.'

'I imagine that the money you stole, if you haven't already spent it, would be out of date now, wouldn't it?'

'Oh, there are ways to make old money work if you know what you're doing. Do you know what you're doing?'

'I know I don't know what you're talking about.'

Goody sighed. 'Ms Grace. Please. Don't treat me like an idiot. I'm willing to come to a mutually satisfactory arrangement with you over this money, phone recordings or no phone recordings. You could do pretty well out of it. I imagine since you're not making movies any more but you're used to having money you're not very good at budgeting. Work with me and you won't need to be.'

Grace paused for a moment. 'Despite what you say, I assume this phone call is being listened to by the prison authorities.'

Goody laughed, not unpleasantly. 'And despite what you say I repeat that the prison authorities don't even know how many phones I've got. They certainly don't know about this one. This conversation is strictly between us, I can assure you.'

'And my recording device. My taxi is waiting. Goodbye, Mr Goody.'

'Don't be a stranger. Seriously.' He sighed again. 'Very seriously.'

Grace pondered the call in the taxi down to the Theatre Royal. She wasn't the kind to dob somebody in so she wasn't going to do anything with the recording, but perhaps it was protection for her.

When the taxi came up Church Street to New Road, she saw a horde of people milling around the theatre entrance and walking away. 'Take me round to the stage door, please.' There she was told about the terrible accidents and that the friend she had come to see perform had gone back to the Grand. Grace headed off there, knowing exactly where in the Grand she would find her friend.

Frank Bilson had been excited about seeing Billie Grahame perform. Gilchrist had heard of her, but her Hollywood fame had been when Gilchrist was just a child. Gilchrist wondered idly if Grahame and Nimue Grace, whom Gilchrist had got to know in recent months, knew each other.

Of course they did. When Gilchrist and Heap arrived the two actresses were sitting at a corner table in the Grand's cocktail bar, heads together deep in conversation. Grace looked up as they approached and gave her big, irresistible grin. She murmured something to Grahame, who observed them closely.

They were both beautiful women, although Grahame was a decade older. Grace, who Gilchrist had met when investigating various deaths linked to her and her wonderful home over the Downs in Plumpton, had a natural beauty and didn't seem ever to wear make-up. Grahame clearly never moved out of the house without putting on the full slap.

Grace stood and kissed both Gilchrist and Heap, which made Heap blush. 'Billie was just telling me about the terrible accident at the theatre earlier. I'll get out of your way and let you ask your questions.'

'Stay, darling, if it's all right with these police officers,' Grahame said. 'I have nothing to hide.'

Grace looked questioningly at Gilchrist, who nodded. 'It's just routine,' she said, perching on a stool on the other side of the table from them. Heap sat on the stool next to her.

'Would you like a drink?' Grace said. Both officers shook their heads. 'Oh, yes, on-duty and all that.'

'Well, I have nothing of interest to say, really,' Grahame said. She touched Grace's arm. 'I never imagined I'd deliver that particular line in real life, Nim.'

'Special circumstances, Billie, special circumstances.'

'I was in my dressing room when the incident occurred. Is that how you say it when someone has copped it – *incident occurred*? I seem to recall that from some cameo I did in a *Death in Paradise*. Have you done that, Nim, or do you not do telly?'

'They asked.'

'You should. The pay is OK and you get a fortnight's holiday on a Caribbean island. You'd be in good company, if you look at who has done it – not just to get that free holiday, of course.'

'It's not my kind of thing – I don't really go for crime stuff.'

'Says the woman who has played a *femme fatale* more times than I can count.'

'That's because you can't count very well, Billie dear. Remember when we did that dreadful play about some mathematics genius together and you just couldn't get that arithmetic in your big speech right?'

'Well, I was distracted by my lust for young Whatshisface, especially when he bent over. Great arse.'

Grace smiled indulgently. 'Anyway, my agent never lets me do telly – thinks it will devalue my *brand* as a movie star or something. I think she's out of touch.'

'Darling, I'll do anything these days if the dosh is right – or there are other attractions.'

Gilchrist thought she should get this back on track. 'You were with Bob Thomas in your dressing room, is that correct?' she said, waving away a waitress, who had come over.

'Talking of other attractions,' Grahame said. 'Young Mr Thomas was keeping me company, yes. You've spoken to him? I trust he was a gentleman?'

You'd know that better than I would, Gilchrist thought. 'Those weights,' she said. 'Were you aware there was any problem with them?'

'Certainly not. It gives me the heebie-jeebies just to think about it. What if *I'd* been standing there when it came down?'

Gilchrist smiled. 'Thank goodness you weren't. Did you know Elvira well?'

'What's that got to do with anything?' Grahame said. 'You're just going through the motions over an accident, aren't you?'

Gilchrist flushed. Grace sat forward. 'You want it to be more, don't you, DI Sarah Gilchrist? You want to investigate another murder.'

Gilchrist blushed some more – she'd be giving Bellamy a run for his money soon – because, of course, Nimue Grace was right.

THREE

Gilchrist got her wish the next morning. 'Rope was severed with a sharp knife,' Bilson said down the phone. 'It looks like it was intentional.'

'It's a bit of a chancy way to kill someone, isn't it?' Gilchrist said. 'Having someone standing in the right place at just the right time to drop a weight on their bonce.'

'Not in theatre or film where the show would be blocked.'

'Blocked?'

'Very specific positions for the lighting and the mise en scène. You need to keep to your mark or stop when you reach it.'

Gilchrist didn't even begin with the mise on scène bit.

'Whoever it was would know exactly where and when Elvira would be standing there,' Bilson continued. 'The bigger question would be how did the killer get on and off the gantry – there is one that runs stage left to stage right above the curtain – without being seen.'

'Nobody backstage noticed anybody up there,' Gilchrist said. 'But then they said none of them would have been looking. They all had jobs to do down below. We need to find a motive first.'

'That's your job, Sarah. I focus on the facts, ma'am. Just the facts.'

'I'm sure that's a quote, Frank, that I've heard from Bellamy before but I'm going to let it go.'

'Very wise, Sarah, very wise. Although I wouldn't have thought Bellamy was old enough to know it. So you'll be interviewing Miss Billie Grahame.'

'Already have, Frank, but, yes, re-interviewing in the light of this news. I met her with Nimue Grace, actually.'

'Nimue Grace *and* Billie Grahame. My cup runneth over.'

'That sounds a bit obscene, Frank. Anything else I need to know – and not about what your cup gets up to?'

'From me? No. From this investigation? Pretty much every-thing, I would have thought.'

Bob Watts stood at the window of his Brighton seafront pent-house, paid for by the money he was left on the death of his bestselling crime-writer father some years earlier. He looked down at the scurrying people on the seafront, battling with a blustery wind, anoraks ballooning and trousers wrapping round skinny legs. Multicoloured lights winked on the attrac-tions on the Palace Pier as the sky slowly darkened.

Watts was wondering how Jimmy Tingley was. Where Tingley was. When his friend went off the grid, he really went off the grid. He just had to hope that all was going well with him.

He was also thinking about getting in touch with Nimue Grace, who wouldn't know he hadn't gone to Canada after all. The circumstances with his ex-wife's new partner had changed abruptly when he had lost money but not his life in a corrupt drugs business with some serious criminals. Watts's erstwhile friend, William Simpson, was also involved and he too had lost money in the drugs operation gone wrong. He was wondering how to bring William Simpson down. Justice for Simpson's various heinous crimes was long overdue.

Jimmy Tingley just wanted to shoot Simpson in the head and have done with it. Watts wasn't happy with that option. Not so much squeamishness, more that he wanted to bring his dam-aging former friend down through legal means. Preferably by hitting him in his pocket, since money was the thing Simpson loved most. Watts just wasn't sure he was bright enough to figure out how to do it.

But he did know one woman who was. One who had worked with Simpson. Margaret Lively, cold-water swimmer at the Serpentine in Hyde Park and hedge fund manager. He hadn't pursued a relationship with her because of their disparity in age and because her occupation was not one he felt sympathetic towards.

But she was a nice, warm woman, which had surprised him for someone who lived in the world of high finance. Perhaps she'd be willing to help? He could phone her. Or he could turn up at the Serpentine in Hyde Park at the crack of dawn, which is where he knew she swam every morning.

The play was cancelled for the next two nights, but the producers assured Brighton audiences it would resume by Friday. The show must go on and all that. In the meantime, Bob Thomas had gone up to London. Billie Grahame was staying on in the Grand. The director, Cat Pinter, was nowhere in evidence. Apparently, this was normal for a play when it had started its run, but not when it needed recasting.

Gilchrist had assumed the director would be there every night, but no. She was told that once the play opens the director generally stays out of the way and the cast are entrusted – with the aid of assistant directors – to keep the play running the way it has been in rehearsal.

'You haven't gone back up to London, Ms Grahame,' Gilchrist said when they were seated in the same bar as the night she'd been with Nimue Grace. Grahame had a large gin and tonic in front of her. Heap sat off to one side.

'Bollocks to that,' Billie Grahame said, making it sound quite sexy in her trademark smoke-damaged voice. 'Let the production pay for my holiday down here.' She leaned forward confidingly, her low-cut blouse revealing her lacy black bra. 'Besides, I've got family members staying in my London flat while I'm down here. The last place I want to be is there with them.'

Gilchrist smiled. 'I'm here to see you again because Elvira's death is being treated as murder.'

'Murder? How? You mean somebody stood up on the gantry and dropped that weight on her head?'

'Sort of, Ms Grahame.'

'And you think it might be me?'

'No – unless you're about to tell me something to the contrary, I was not expecting that you had shinned up onto the gantry to commit the crime. However, at the moment we are simply trying to establish a motive for the crime and wondered if you could help with anything you might have observed.'

Grahame sipped her drink, then dabbed her lips with a napkin, smudging her scarlet lipstick.

'I didn't mix with her, or the other young actors. Or that daft director, for that matter.'

'You weren't happy in this production?'

'Well, you don't miss a thing, do you? I can see why you made detective inspector.' Grahame smiled and patted Gilchrist's arm, presumably to offset her rudeness. Gilchrist still bridled.

'You mentioned the director, Cat Pinter?' Gilchrist said calmly.

'All of twenty-five and already full of shit. Or, perhaps, *therefore* full of shit. I probably was at that age, although I think I had a harder head on my shoulders. Except when it came to men, of course.'

'The director?' Gilchrist said.

'Don't call her that – a director – to her face. She's a *theatre-maker*, don't you know.' Grahame saw Gilchrist's puzzled look. 'Meant to mean you're more creative, I think. Just as these days nobody programmes a film festival or an arts programme or even a fashion show: they *curate* it.'

Gilchrist nodded. 'I see. About Cat Pinter, I mean. But you don't get on?'

'We get on fine – I do what I'm told. I just thought most of what I was told made no sense. Always have obeyed directors, unlike Nimue. She has nothing to be embarrassed about. All of my generation knew to put DRR on the bottom of photographs we sent out when we were trying to get work at the start of our careers.'

'DRR?'

'Director's Rights Respected.' Gilchrist obviously looked puzzled. 'It was code, dear. If you give me a job, you can have sex with me. Nimue never did anything like that – aside from the fact she got her break pretty much out of drama school and never looked back, she wouldn't have anyway. She's never been that kind of woman.'

'I think Sir Ian McKellan talked about DRR in the press,' Heap murmured.

'Ah, Ian – bless him. Lovely man. I was in the Shakespeare film he shot down here at the Royal Pavilion with Kristen and Maggie and Annette Bening. And Robert Downey Jr – hasn't he done well? Ever the Comeback Kid.'

'Had Elvira made any enemies during the production?' Gilchrist said, trying to get back to her investigation.

'I didn't mix much with the other actors as I said. Not my snootiness – theirs. It became obvious there was a bit of a youth cult thing going on with this play. In my day, young and old would hang out together. Not in this production.

'In this play, it's my character who is the most sympathetic, but Cat blocked it out so that the three younger actors undercut my most moving moments by sneering at me – and making the audience complicit in that by winking at them as they were doing so.'

'I'm not really a theatre-goer . . .' Gilchrist began but Grahame wasn't listening.

'Every night before the show in those first days,' she continued, 'the director insisted on us coming in an hour early to do a group exercise. We sat on the floor and did breathing exercises and contorted for half an hour. Well, everyone else did. I'd nip out for a fag and pop back in at the end. None of them noticed.'

'Was it the director who made you unhappy?' Gilchrist cut in, trying to stop the other woman going off at a tangent.

'The *theatre-maker*, Cat? Very nice young woman, if eccentric. But she couldn't direct traffic. She could never make her mind up what she wanted. She kept changing bits, adding bits, even when we'd been running a couple of weeks. That's just not done.'

'I was surprised to hear the director doesn't come to every performance,' Gilchrist said.

'Oh, they're usually on to the next job. The ADs – assistant directors – stay with the show and the director occasionally bobs back in if things are going askew. Except, as I say, Cat wouldn't leave the show alone for the first two weeks.'

'You said she's eccentric. In what way?'

'I think you'll find that out for yourself when you interview her.'

'Anything to add about Elvira?'

'She insisted she was non-binary or non-gender specific or whatever it is people are saying these days. She told me I was a cis, which sounds like something that needs lancing. When I looked it up, she wasn't telling me anything I didn't already know – that I'm a woman born and bred. But she made it sound as if there was something wrong with that.' Grahame sighed. 'I'm so glad I'm not growing up now during this self-inflicted sexual— excuse me – *gender* confusion.'

'Some see it as gender liberation,' Heap said quietly.

Grahame looked him up and down but said nothing. She finished her gin and tonic and smiled at Gilchrist and Heap. 'Nimue told me you and this young man are friends of hers.'

'I wouldn't go so far as to say that,' Gilchrist said.

'You don't like her?' Grahame said.

'I didn't say that,' Gilchrist said. 'I meant I wouldn't presume to say we were friends.'

'Well, she does presume, so that makes you friends whether you like it or not.'

'You've known her long?' Heap said.

'You must know that actresses as they get older hate to be asked about anything to do with time passing or periods of time. Yes, we met and became friends on a film shooting in Argentina, in the most beautiful circumstances. The production was camped – I believe glamped is the modern expression, since we were in very luxurious tents – in the middle of nowhere on the campus . . . no, Pampas.

'Sound travelled far further than one realized. I'm afraid I was going through a rather loopy phase – for reasons I'm not sure I can explain, even to myself, except that I'd spent a lot of time on another film with Sarah Miles, who was into this stuff. Anyway, I was meditating, practising celibacy and drinking my own urine. Except that Nimue took me aside to point out that if I wanted to be taken seriously about the celibacy I needed to curb my noisy demonstrations of pleasure at being comprehensively rogered by one of the other leads in my tent every night.' She spread her hands. 'My friendship with Nimue has lasted far longer than that inconsequential fling.'

Late in the evening, Watts was still thinking about Margaret Lively and William Simpson when his phone rang. He'd got a new phone and hadn't yet changed the factory setting ring, so it was more yodel than ring.

'Hello?' he said, turning away from the window with his glass of tequila.

'Bob? It's Graham Goody. How are you?'

'I'm fine. This is unexpected.'

'How's Jimmy?'

'In the wind,' Bob said. 'To what do I owe the pleasure?'

'I'm planning ahead. I wondered if, when I get out, you might be willing to introduce me to your squeeze, the lovely Nimue Grace.'

Watts sighed. 'She's not my *squeeze*.'

'Taking it slow, are you? I'm fine, by the way. Thanks for asking.'

'You're not out for years, are you?'

'Well, I'm working on reducing that timing.'

'Really? Prison breaks are frowned on you know.'

'Oh, I didn't mean that. Using legal means.'

Watts let that one go. 'Why do you want to meet her?' he said.

'Oh, not to step on your toes. I wouldn't dream of doing anything like that. I'm just an admirer of her work. But a friend of mine is thinking about buying that crook Said Farzi's old gaff next door and we wanted to talk to her about that.'

'We?'

'Well, I thought I might buy into the Sussex wine boom.'

'You have that kind of money? Crime does pay then?'

'I'm just a canny investor, that's all. But, yeah, and so I would like to meet her more casually than just knocking on her door.'

'What's going on, Graham?'

'Absolutely nothing, Mr Watts. I've told you. Plus, I'm just a bit of a culture vulture and she is culture writ large – and, admittedly, she looks like a goddess. Some women cloy the appetites they feed and all that, you know, Bob.'

'That last bit went right over my head,' Watts said. 'And it's nothing to do with your stolen money being found in her lake a few months ago?'

'Look,' Goody said. 'Let's meet for a drink when I'm out – your treat, of course, since you're really rolling in it –

and we can catch up and I can explain, so you're not so suspicious.'

'I'm suspicious about how you're planning to get out sooner rather than later. I thought, even with the word I put in, you had a few more years to go.'

'Well, when there was no lightning bolt striking me the last time, I gave someone up. I thought I'd make a bit of a habit of it. Only scumbags, mind; no honest criminals.'

'Where are you going to be based?'

'I thought I'd stay in this area. Keep an eye on my investment, if I make one. Catch up with the Henfield ex-SAS boys. Are you planning any outings with the boys? Count me in, if you are.'

'Really?'

'Come on, Bobby. You know why I went into crime – well, aside from the money. The adrenaline. Don't you miss it?'

Watts poured himself another large tequila, noting the scars on his knuckles. 'Not really.'

'You mean you find your work as police commissioner – and who knows what that work is? – gets your adrenaline going, do you?'

'Not really. But listen, isn't there a queue of people behind you waiting to use this phone.'

Goody chuckled. 'The other day in the yard warders found three dead rats, intestines removed, bellies stitched back up after they'd been stuffed with drugs and mobile phones. They had been thrown over the wall. They used to use pigeons. But that's old school.'

'So how do they do it these days, if it's not rats?' Watts said. 'Drones, I suppose.'

'That's right, Bobby. That and paying off guards. You don't have much of a clue about the current state of prisons, do you?'

'I know it's pretty dire.'

'For some maybe. I'm lying on my bed in my cell watching a movie on my laptop – have you seen those old Jean-Pierre Melville gangster movies? Love them. Not for Alain Delon – he's just a blank. I love them *despite* Alain Delon. I know them almost by heart. And I'm using my mobile – one of my many mobiles – and I do have Alexa.'

'Use one of them to call me when you're out. Let's have a drink in Brighton.'

'And my introduction to Nimue Grace?'

'Just call me when you get out.'

FOUR

S arah Gilchrist was sitting on the balcony of her flat in a secluded Brighton square with a pot of coffee and a plate of chocolate digestives – well, it was breakfast time. She dipped a biscuit in her coffee and looked out across the trees in full bloom. There was honeysuckle with a divine scent growing along the balcony next door.

She'd been feeling crotchety for days and she thought she knew why. She'd been growing tired of ostrich egg omelettes and her time in the country. Did that mean she was growing tired of Mark Harrison, the ostrich farmer in Plumpton she'd been having a relationship with for the past couple of months? Even as she wondered at the phrase *the ostrich farmer she'd been having a relationship with* she considered how surreal life could be.

She'd been missing working the streets of Brighton. It was beautiful on the Sussex Downs and county lines drugs had become a major issue in the area, but she felt there was more to be done here, especially since most of the drugs in the county were coming out of the city.

Bellamy Heap was quite happy operating over the other side of the Downs. He already lived with her friend, Kate Simpson, in Lewes.

Although, Kate was a worry at the moment. Gilchrist didn't really know what was going on with her any more. She'd never quite understood Kate's determination to swim the Channel and now she was off in Yorkshire doing a creative writing course.

Bellamy hadn't been his usual ebullient self since Kate headed north and Gilchrist wondered if they'd split up. She didn't feel able to ask him but was dying to ask Kate. With that thought, she rooted around for her mobile.

'Kate – it's Sarah. Just checking that you're OK.'

'Sarah – this is a surprise. I'm on a writing course, you know.

I shouldn't really even be answering my phone.' Gilchrist said nothing. 'Why would I not be OK?' Kate added.

'No reason at all. I was just checking. How is the writing going?'

'Writing is fine, thanks.'

'And the writing centre?'

'Great. It's Sylvia Plath's old place.'

As if she knew who Sylvia Plath was. She took a stab at appearing knowledgeable anyway. 'Not waving but drowning?'

'That's Stevie Smith.'

'Near,' Gilchrist said, and they both laughed. 'What's happening with you and Bellamy?'

'Sarah! It's not like you to ask questions like that. Especially over breakfast.'

'Sorry – are you with other people? Can you talk?'

'I'm out on the terraces looking at the view – goodness, it's rugged round here. And nobody else is up. We all had a bit of a late night last night.'

'Sounds great. But, well, I care about you both and I'm getting sentimental in my old age. Everything OK?'

'What about you and Ostrich Man?' Kate said.

'How many ostrich omelettes can one girl eat?' Gilchrist said with a laugh. 'Lovely guy but I don't think it's going to go anywhere.'

There was silence on the line, then: 'I needed some time alone, just for myself,' Kate said. 'This writing course seemed the perfect opportunity. Bellamy understands.'

'Bellamy would,' Gilchrist murmured. 'Your mum's death and not achieving the Channel Swim – through no fault of your own, let me hastily add – hit you hard, I know.'

Kate was quiet for a moment then: 'Harder than *I* knew,' she said quietly. Then she added in brighter tones, 'Look, I'll be back in a few days. Let's grab a cocktail or two at whatever the latest hip, shiny bar is in Brighton and be girlie.'

Gilchrist smiled down the phone. 'You're on.'

When she hung up, Gilchrist began thinking again about the theatre deaths and group panic that ensued. She'd had her own experience of that kind of panic on Oxford Street in London just before Christmas a couple of years earlier.

She'd been in London for a meeting and had managed to get to John Lewis before it closed. It was Black Friday, so Oxford Street was teeming. She was in the basement getting some kitchen stuff – the jug of her cafetière had broken for one thing, so she needed a replacement – when suddenly a rush of people came down the escalator and across the basement, knocking aside bystanders as they piled into a room at the back where they all cowered.

Gilchrist pushed through the crowd towards the escalator as a bunch of staff led yet more people into the basement. She collared one of them. 'I'm police. What's going on?'

'Terrorists on Oxford Street. The police out there have told everybody to get off the street, so everybody is coming in here. It's pandemonium upstairs.'

'Is there a back way out of the store from down here?'

'Staff entrance – that's where we've been told to lead people.'

'Sounds like you have a procedure,' Gilchrist said. 'You're doing a good job. Let me stay with you and help.' Seeing the young man struggle with his own panic, she'd quickly decided that the trained police upstairs wouldn't need any help from her and that she'd be more useful down here.

By then, more people had rushed downstairs. She and the young man – his name was Michael, she ascertained – led a crocodile line of shoppers up two floors using a flight of stairs at the back. Double doors at the side of the store were open and a couple of staff were directing people out to the backstreet behind the store.

Out there it was chaos as people were pouring out the rear exits of Debenhams and Selfridges and every other store on this side of Oxford Street. Most were running, barrelling past those who were slower. The street was littered with discarded shopping bags from the different stores.

Gilchrist helped up an older woman who had been knocked over by one surge. She led her to an office building on a street heading north behind John Lewis where she could see people in the foyer looking out at the chaos.

'I was in Debenhams when the bombs went off in there,' the woman said.

'You saw it happen?' Gilchrist said.

The woman shook her head. 'I was on the first floor. I heard two loud crashes on the ground floor.'

A sudden surge of people almost dislodged them from their position outside the office block. Gilchrist rattled the doors and a young woman in a smart business suit came across the foyer and let them in.

'The first floor might be safer,' she said, her voice quavering. 'There are hot drinks there too.'

Gilchrist helped the woman – her name was Phoebe and she'd come in from north London for Christmas shopping – up the stairs. The woman was limping. She saw Gilchrist looking.

'I bruised my knee when I fell,' she said.

On the first floor, Gilchrist sat her with a couple of distressed Asian girls in head scarves speaking hurriedly into their phones, each of them on the verge of tears. Gilchrist went over to a kitchen area and made Phoebe a sweet tea – the girls had cans of something loaded with caffeine.

When she got back one of the girls, who had the most beautiful doe eyes, turned to her and said: 'We heard gunshots in the store, really near.'

Gilchrist nodded and took out her mobile. She googled breaking news and the BBC had a brief report that there has been an incident at Oxford Circus Tube station and gunshots had been fired in the surrounding streets and counterterrorism police were on the scene in force.

'You're safe here,' she said. 'The police have blanketed the area.'

She went back downstairs and the woman with the quavering voice reluctantly let her back out into what was now a quieter street. 'I think the worst is over,' Gilchrist said to her. 'You've done very well here.'

As she walked north away from Oxford Street, she assumed the panic was over or simply that everyone shopping on Oxford Street had left the area by now. She went into a Pret on the first corner she came to and ordered an almond slice and a hot chocolate. Nothing wrong with a sugar rush in such circumstances.

It was only when she got her purse out to pay she realized she'd stuffed the replacement cafetière jug she'd found in

John Lewis in her bag. Detective Inspector Sarah Gilchrist: shoplifter.

Then another stampede of people came down the street. Two male members of staff quickly closed a massive wooden door at the entrance and bolted it while a giggly young woman behind the counter directed everyone into the basement kitchen.

A Swedish girl was sobbing into her phone. Gilchrist googled the BBC news again. No developments: no deaths, no sightings of the terrorists.

'It's OK,' Gilchrist said, when the girl put her phone back in her pocket. 'I'm not sure anything has actually happened.'

'I heard gunshots in the street,' she sobbed. 'I was just letting my parents know I'm safe.'

Gilchrist frowned. She had been listening for explosions and gunfire when she'd stumbled out of John Lewis and had heard nothing then, nor on the way here. She munched her almond slice and drank her hot chocolate as she looked online again. Still no further developments.

She went back upstairs and persuaded the staff to let her out, then walked parallel to Oxford Street back towards Oxford Circus, realizing as she went that she hadn't paid for her hot chocolate and almond slice either.

In a pub doorway, she heard a man, drawing heavily on a cigarette, talking into his phone. 'Yeah, two of them have taken twenty hostages in Topshop . . .'

When Gilchrist reached the north end of Regent Street, there was a police cordon some twenty yards away. She went over to a bunch of armed policemen and identified herself.

'Developments?' she said.

A young, bearded policeman shrugged. 'Nothing.'

'The hostage situation in Topshop?'

'Oh, we haven't heard that one before.' He called over to the others. 'Hey, guys, apparently we have a hostage situation at Topshop.' They all laughed.

Gilchrist left them and continued to walk parallel to Oxford Street until she got to Tottenham Court Road. That Tube station too was closed off, so she hopped into a cab, which went a circuitous but glittery route through Covent Garden to drop her off at Temple, where she got the District line to Victoria and her train home to Brighton.

By the time she got home, the BBC had more on the story. An unidentified incident had happened at Oxford Circus Tube on one of the crowded platforms. Panic had ensued there and London Transport Police, following the anti-terrorist procedure drilled into them in recent years, had evacuated the station, leading to more panic among its customers.

The sense of urgency instilled into the crowd as they emerged on to Oxford Street, only to see a phalanx of armed Metropolitan Police bellowing at them to get off the streets as quickly as they could, would have increased the terror.

Gilchrist could see it now: all these terrified people rushing into the department stores, panicking the people in there. The bombs going off? The gunshots fired? Displays crashing over as the mob hurtled through the ground floors of these stores. One crash is pretty much like another to people predisposed to be nervous about terrorism.

The next morning, over a coffee made in her nice new cafetière jug, she learned that not a single bullet cartridge had been found anywhere around Oxford Circus. No bomb had gone off anywhere. Nobody had been killed, although a number had been injured by the mindless mob. No terrorist had been seen, let alone arrested. And later it transpired that the whole thing had started with a punch-up between two strangers on a crowded platform with people pushing other people to get out of the way of it.

Gilchrist had read about crowd behaviour on sinking ferries or in disaster scenarios before but to experience it at a low level had been quite an eye-opener for her. She had vowed never to forget.

FIVE

'Intriguing surprise you turning up at the Serps again,' Margaret Lively said. 'I thought that after your friend's Channel attempt you had eschewed cold-water swimming. Or did you have another motive to come here this morning?'

They were in the café beside the Serpentine in Hyde Park. Bob Watts was huddling over a green tea trying to stop shivering – his body had found it a shock going into the cold water after a few months' absence. Lively looked over the rim of her coffee mug at Watts, an amused look on her face. 'Is it because you finally found something original to say about my last name?'

Watts smiled. 'It's lovely to see you again.' And it was. She was a bright, attractive woman.

As if guessing what he was thinking when he looked at her, she said: 'Have I aged sufficiently for you to have another go?'

'Would you like me to have another go?' Watts said.

'I'm still waiting for the first go,' Lively said, then flushed.

Watts smiled. He had no idea how to play this. He didn't want to lead this young woman on but he did need her help.

'What's your relationship with William Simpson like these days?' he said.

Lively looked disappointed. 'Ah. I see. It's not me you're interested in, it's your – what did you call him once – *erstwhile* friend. I must admit I'm a little hurt.'

'Please don't be – you misunderstand me. I've had time to think that perhaps I was silly worrying about the age gap.'

'It took you a lot of time to think that out. Maybe you're not as bright as I think you are.'

'I'm undoubtedly not as bright as *anyone* thinks I am. But the situation was complicated by the reason I was going to Canada. I was trying to screw up a dodgy deal William Simpson was involved in.'

'I thought you were going to get your ex-wife out of a fix?' Lively was watching him intently.

'By screwing up William Simpson's deal with some very bad men.'

'And did you succeed?'

'I didn't end up doing anything – the circumstances abruptly changed – but the deal did go south.'

Lively tilted her head. 'And you want to know why? I don't get involved in dodgy deals, Robert. I'm surprised you think I would.'

Watts sighed. 'I'm sorry, Margaret. I didn't mean that.' He showed her his palms. 'Look, I do need help, I don't mind admitting that. But that's not why I'm here. As you've probably guessed, I'm not very good at financial stuff. I want to bring Simpson down, but I don't know how to do it.'

Lively drained her coffee cup. 'One of the things that intrigue me about you, Bob, is that you look like a pleasant white-collar worker.' She pointed at his scarred knuckles. 'But the first time I looked at your hands, I saw these scars. I guess I should have noticed the way you walk, the way you hold yourself.'

Watts couldn't think of anything to say.

'But I am questioning your intelligence. Why are you telling me that you want to bring down a business associate of mine without having any idea what my relationship with William Simpson is?'

Watts leaned forward and took Lively's hand. She didn't resist.

'Because I've decided you're a good person and, as you said, you wouldn't be involved in anything dodgy. Nor will you want anything to do with William Simpson once I've told you *all* about him.'

Lively sat back and looked into her empty coffee cup. 'Sounds like I'm gonna need another coffee. You're sounding very patronizing, so you're buying, I presume.' She looked at her watch. 'Better still, buy me lunch in Soho.'

Gilchrist and Heap took the train up to London to visit Elvira's flat. They had tried and failed to locate Cat Pinter. She was theoretically between jobs, but she wasn't at home in Stoke Newington and none of the crew knew where she was. The ADs were dealing with the two replacement actors. In Cat Pinter's absence, they had ditched the Zimmer frame.

Gilchrist and Heap had already spoken to Tom Marigold's parents and girlfriend about the awful accident and discreetly tried to find out anything they might know about Elvira or her situation. They knew nothing. Marigold's girlfriend had wondered if Tom Marigold and Elvira might have been having an affair, as they were close, but Marigold had reassured her that it was simply part of 'the process'.

'Blooming actors,' Gilchrist said, as their train came over the Thames and they both looked out at yet more steel-and-glass high-rise constructions on either side of the river. 'Feeling they have to find an excuse to have it off with somebody else in the cast when they're already in a relationship.'

'It's just the language they use, ma'am – they're just like you and me really.'

'Speak for yourself,' Gilchrist said, surprised by her own sourness. 'They're nothing like me.'

Elvira lived in an official squat in a former bank just off Oxford Street. Gilchrist didn't know such things as official squats existed, but apparently a kind of alternative property company specialized in running these places for artists of various sorts.

Elvira lived alone in the basement. A shared bathroom was on the ground floor. The young, attractive lesbian couple living on that floor had nothing to tell Gilchrist. They sat together on the sofa and looked at each other to check that what each was saying made sense. They spoke cautiously, presumably not wanting to be misunderstood or, perhaps, misquoted. Gilchrist wondered if they had had a bad experience with the police at some point.

They didn't see Elvira much. She just seemed to bob in and out. As far as they knew, Elvira had no friends visiting and didn't mix with them. She was intense, they both agreed on that, and lived in her own world, most of the time. Glances at each other and nods. Didn't spend much time in that bathroom – a shared smile this time.

'She did mention her parents were dead and she had no siblings,' the red-haired one of them said as the other nodded.

(Gilchrist couldn't for the life of her remember either of these women's names, which was a worry.)

'She was posh. She spoke – what's it called? – received pronunciation,' the other one said. 'But then she was an actress – some of them can be very good with them, can't they? That Jodie Comer does that brilliant eastern European accent and then switches to a perfect snooty one in *Killing Eve* – but have you heard her being interviewed in real life? She's a total Scouser.'

'Total,' her partner said.

'Did she say how she'd got the part in the play she was doing?' Heap asked.

'Didn't know she was in a play. In the West End?'

'Perhaps eventually,' Heap said. 'And she never mentioned a Cat Pinter?'

'We told you,' either or both said, 'she never mentioned anything except putting a new loo roll in the bathroom or something.'

Gilchrist and Heap thanked them and walked in silence back to the Tube. Everything pointed to Elvira being alone as well as being a loner. No indication of her sexuality, although Gilchrist had got used to the fact that sexuality had become more readily fluid among many young people. Plus, the remark Billie Grahame had reported suggested Elvira had been questioning her gender.

Gilchrist scratched her head. How did Elvira get cast? Had she met Cat before? Did they meet before production started? Surely they must have done.

DC Sylvia Wade, who was coming on nicely as an intelligent, thoughtful police officer, had already interviewed all the stagehands and everyone else who had been backstage at the theatre for a second time after their initial interviews. The interviews had come up blank. On the train back to Brighton, Gilchrist looked down the list of names and read the statements again. Well, almost blank. She phoned Wade from the train – she and Heap were in an empty carriage so she put the phone on speaker.

'I can't find Elvira's birth certificate, ma'am,' Sylvia Wade said apologetically.

'Does Equity not have anything?' Heap asked, referring to the actors' union.

'She's not a member,' Wade said.

'But I thought—'

'Me too, sir, but that was the old days. Like in every other industry the union has lost its grip. Where before you couldn't get an acting job unless you were in Equity and you couldn't get an Equity card unless you were acting, nowadays there is no requirement to be in the union.'

'So she is from abroad?' Heap said. 'The name Elvira might tip that, I suppose.'

'If it isn't just a stage name,' Wade said. 'I've circulated her details to Interpol and individual European crime agencies – while we still can be considered equal partners in them.'

'No politics for us, DC Wade,' Heap said quietly.

'I know that, sir,' Wade said. 'Anyway, nothing back yet.'

'If she is from another country, I wonder if it's some kind of vendetta from abroad,' Gilchrist said. 'What have we got on nationality? When and where she entered the country?'

'Nothing. No record of her entering the country under the name of Elvira Wright. And no passport to be found as yet.'

'Maybe she was an illegal, smuggled in. That increases the chances of a motive. Got into a debt with the smugglers she couldn't pay back. There was nothing in her hotel room, was there?'

'Clothes and a washbag and a book about Stanislavski – the Method acting person, ma'am. No phone; no computer.'

'Get SOCO up to the London flat, get the usual permissions from the Met, see if they can find a computer there, or – if there is a God – diaries and letters and great DNA.'

'Will do, ma'am.'

'Any word on Cat Pinter? Has she surfaced?'

'No sign of her. Her parents aren't close to her. They haven't seen her for a couple of years but they claim to be OK with that.'

'Nice parents,' Gilchrist muttered.

'We don't know what triggered that split – they didn't say – or rather denied there was a split.'

'So are we putting out a Missing Person's alert for Cat Pinter, the director? Correction: *theatre-maker.*'

'Already done, ma'am,' Wade said. 'But as yet nothing.'

'Listen, Sylvia, one of the women working backstage' – she scanned down the list of names – 'Flick Steadman, props girl, said the only person she'd ever seen up on the gantry was Cat Pinter, but she didn't know if she'd seen her there that evening. It's probably nothing since nobody else saw Cat Pinter in the theatre that night but can you follow up on that?'

Anything was worth a try. The investigation was stalling. Nothing to go on and nowhere to go. Gilchrist wasn't happy about this. At all. She liked to take things through to a conclusion, if she could.

As if reading her mind, Heap said: 'Let's wait to see what SOCO comes up with, ma'am.'

SIX

Margaret Lively sat across from Bob Watts in a crowded pop-up in Soho, both of them tucking into Padron peppers. 'So you want to get William Simpson?'

'He's overdue,' Watts said.

'What happened in Canada?'

'I didn't go in the end.'

'So you said, but that doesn't explain what happened.'

'The situation changed.'

She nodded. 'I heard William had pulled out of the syndicate over there,' she said. 'Something to do with a changed situation here.'

The syndicate William Simpson was part of included the criminal gang and Watts's ex-wife's current partner. But William Simpson had also been about to go into business with Said Farzi, the Morocco and Sussex-based marijuana manufacturer – and modern slaver – who had been Grace's threatening neighbour until he went on the run.

When Farzi's UK operation was dismantled so effectively by Sarah Gilchrist and Bellamy Heap, Simpson had cut his losses in Sussex largely out of self-preservation.

Watts nodded at Lively. 'A business setback for him in Sussex.'

'Because of you?'

Watts shook his head. 'Because of him. And Canada didn't pan out. The great Canadian drug experiment hasn't worked, so there was nothing for William Simpson to invest in unless he wanted to go totally illegal. It had proved too expensive for the company he had backed to operate.'

'You mean the government totally legalizing cannabis hasn't panned out? But they only did it in 2018.'

'That's right. Companies invested millions expecting to make more millions. Taxes from sales would benefit the Commonwealth. By now most companies have shed half their staff or closed down altogether. The aim was to ensure people who used cannabis were getting good stuff that wouldn't harm them – well, that wouldn't harm them with extra junk stuffed in there to bulk it up. And it would cut down on drug-related crime, of course.'

'But they overhyped it? Created a bubble that has burst?'

'Exactly. Multibillion dollar stock market losses, massive job losses. If you were very smart and got in at the start and out quickly, you made a very tidy sum but everyone else got the dregs.'

'We call it vulture capitalism. If you're quick, you make a lot of money but the fallout for everyone else is catastrophic.'

'As it was, although since most investors were in it for a quick greedy buck but weren't quick enough you might argue they got what they deserved.'

'Bob, I think you misunderstand the essential nature of capitalism.'

He laughed. 'Probably.'

'We saw it in the dotcom boom in the nineties. Or the gold rushes in the nineteenth century – when you were just a young'un, Bob.'

He laughed at that unexpected jab. 'Thanks very much. But, yes, that's exactly what happened. Investors pumped money into massive cannabis farms to meet the anticipated massive demand. And there was no massive demand.'

'But why?'

'Uncoordinated rollout as best I can tell. The growers grew tons of good stuff, but they couldn't get it to market. There weren't enough government-approved retail shops. There were lots of eager buyers, but they couldn't easily get it. Then the pricing was high because there was the tax, massive overheads, compliance with all the safety requirements. It cost a fortune just storing the cannabis in massive vaults on the cannabis farms. And growers had to pay a high price for security.

'Meanwhile, the illegal market kept its prices low, what they sold was readily available and they actually had a wider range of product. So users have mostly stayed with them, leaving the big cannabis corporations with stockpiles of stuff they can't sell.'

'Maybe there's another factor in it too. Most people who smoke dope like to think they are a bit hip, probably anti-authoritarian. Maybe they found buying it legally just too boring.'

'That's a strong possibility,' Watts said. 'But do you mind me asking what kind of business you and Simpson exactly did together?'

'Hedge-funderish kind of business,' Lively said. 'Do you really want the details?'

Watts shook his head. 'I suppose I want to know what your relationship with him is.'

'Strictly business.'

Watts sat back. 'I assumed that – I'm sorry, I didn't mean anything else.'

Lively grinned at him. 'Uncomfortable, Bob?' She picked up a pepper and held it in front of him. 'Instead of your foot, do you want to stuff another pepper into your mouth?' Watts nodded, a rueful look on his face. Lively took a sip of her wine, still grinning. 'Money laundering,' she said.

'That's what you were doing together?'

'Don't dig yourself a deeper hole, Bob. No, that's how you get him.'

'He launders money for whom?'

'For *whom*? You are wonderfully old-fashioned, aren't you? Well, let's see – pretty much anyone who is despicable around the world. In a small way.'

'But I assume he does that in a tax haven somewhere.'

'Well, you'd assume wrong. But look, haven't we talked about enough business. I'll explain later.' She picked up the menu. 'Let's choose a main course? We need to keep up our strength.'

'We do?'

'Well, yes.' She gave him an up-from-under look. 'It could be a long afternoon.'

Nimue Grace sat very still watching the two green woodpeckers using their long beaks to get ant larvae from her lawn. She knew they were nesting in one of her trees, but she didn't know which one. She glanced over at the low bushes under which tiny plump wrens were living.

There was the constant murmur of bees in the cherry blossom. Two crows were chasing off a predator bird in the sky, whirling round him as he swerved and dipped to get rid of them.

She loved this garden. She didn't want to lose it, but she was running out of money. And what the hell was she going to do about Graham Goody? She had the money he had stolen well enough hidden, but it would be no use to her if she couldn't convert it and he clearly wasn't going to give up.

Should she do the deal so she could keep this place? She shifted her Edwardian letter opener from hand to hand.

She didn't know how to get money any other way. Secretly, she'd assumed when she sensationally quit Hollywood that, if the time felt right, she'd be able to resume her career there. That's hubris for you. How wrong she'd been. She was forgotten. The waters had closed over her. Other beautiful talented women had come along.

Now all she was offered was British telly. She'd said to Billie Grahame that her agent didn't want her to do TV but actually it was Grace herself. It was a snobbishness in her that couldn't quite give up the fact she'd been a movie star and she felt that doing TV would be such a comedown. Her agent, cooing sympathetically, had once said that Grace was quite right and that she mustn't devalue her *brand*. 'Although Glenda Jackson did a telly not so long ago, dear.'

'Well, she's nearly ninety and it was about dementia. I'm not sure I'm quite there yet.'

'Just saying.'

She didn't know about being a brand, but she did know that she didn't want to do any old rubbish – well, unless it paid really well, as it had in Hollywood. She was cross with herself that she had squandered all that money – or, rather, that she had allowed that Spanish creep, who had moved so sneakily into her life at her time of greatest vulnerability, to spend it. And, indeed, steal it. Call her cold-hearted but she was glad he was dead. The bastard.

She had some voice-over ad work on offer. That kind of work appealed if it was not going to be heard in the UK or the US. She giggled about how, when it got to the boring rules and regulations bits at the end of an ad, the voice-over artist had to sprint towards the speedy denouement of *Terms and Conditions Apply*.

She'd heard that Martin Scorsese had been paid millions to do *The Audition*, an ad that was only shown in Asia promoting casinos in Manila, Macau and Japan. The twenty-minute ad, which, of course, ended up on YouTube so was seen round the world, was a shameless piece of money-grubbing, in her view, but if the principles used the money for their various charities, all well and good. The principles were De Niro, DiCaprio and Brad Pitt, each also getting paid millions for appearing in it. Now that kind of work she could do. Except she was too old – Charlize Theron got the gig with Adam Driver and Brad Pitt doing the Breitling watch ad for the eastern market. God knows how much they got paid for that piece of attractive-looking garbage.

She was naturally an optimistic person but she couldn't see any optimistic angle here. Grace closed her eyes. When she opened them an oleaginous-looking man in a smart suit and tie was standing at the side entrance to the garden.

SEVEN

Bob Watts and Margaret Lively got out of bed around five. She got a bottle of wine out of the fridge and took it out to a table in a small courtyard at the rear of her house. Watts joined her there.

'You were telling me about money laundering.'

'Is that the end of pillow talk, then?' she said, arching her eyebrows.

'Get me a pillow and I'll see what I can do.'

She grinned impishly. 'Later, perhaps.'

He raised his glass. 'Here's to later.'

'OK – you mentioned that you thought Simpson would work out of tax havens. Didn't you know Britain has the disgraceful dishonour of being the money-laundering capital of the world?'

'I didn't know that.'

Lively swirled her wine around in her glass.

'HSBC outdid itself in the late twentieth century cleaning up Latin American drug cartel money. It got fined $1.9 billion by the US government for that in 2012. Then, Danske Bank in Denmark passed 200 billion euros through its Estonian branch between 2007 and 2015, mostly from Soviet Union mafiosi, some allegedly linked to Putin. But even in that, Britain was key. In the Danish bank scandal, all the dodgy accounts were registered with companies in the UK.'

'So how is the money cleaned up?'

'Electronic transfer – and that means a bank account with a name attached.'

Watts nodded. 'And that means shell companies. I still thought such companies were all off-shore – Virgin Islands and so on.'

She sipped her wine and gave a small smile. 'Used to be they were. But not these days. A whistle-blower about this scandal called the UK "an absolute disgrace". It never gets mentioned by the Government or the Opposition – almost as if it's understood that all this money sloshing through Britain is good for the economy.'

'But how can it slosh through without being spotted?'

Lively sat back. 'There's a huge loophole in the way we register companies in the UK. Think of it as a black hole into which criminals can put in billions to make it disappear – except that, unlike a black hole, it does come out the other side.'

'What's the loophole?'

'Britain doesn't bother much with due diligence when a company is registered at Companies House, even though it insists that places like the British Virgin Islands do thorough checks. Here, you register for under twenty pounds and pretty much all you have to do is provide a name and address.'

'Well, the name and address is the giveaway, isn't it?' Watts said.

'Not at all – because nobody checks. Companies House doesn't follow up on the names and addresses it is given. It doesn't have the capacity, given there are millions of companies registered. For all you know some crook could have registered dozens of shady companies using the name Bob Watts and your address.'

Watts also sat back. 'Extraordinary.'

'A few years back the government made it compulsory to name the individual who owns the company – that person is known as the PSC, the Person with Significant Control. But nobody checks on them. I read an investigation in the *Guardian* that showed PSCs were often just strings of random letters. And an anti-corruption campaign group found a few thousand of the PSCs were children under the age of two.'

'That seems pretty easy to spot if you're looking,' Watts said.

'True, but nobody is looking. However, the cannier ones do try to make it plausible. They use a real name – somebody else's, obviously. A real address – ditto. They say they have audited accounts – they don't have to file them – and give the name of the accountancy firm they have used. That name they've picked at random after googling such firms.'

'And that's it?'

'Pretty much.'

'But hang on, what about the banks? Don't they check?'

'Not when your company is registered at Companies House. That's good enough for them.'

'And William Simpson is implicated in this?'

'Almost certainly. He only just escaped implication in the scandal around the money laundering of the ex-dictator of the Ukraine. But his consulting company is involved with all kinds of dodgy regimes and corporations.'

'And you're implicated too?'

'Not at all,' she said indignantly. 'We were both engaged in a project for the West Pier years ago but that came to nothing and then various vague projects were discussed.'

Watts drained his glass and gave her a long look. 'Does this constitute *later*, do you think?'

She drained her glass too. 'I would certainly hope so.'

'Who the fuck are you?' Grace demanded of the man who had appeared at the garden's side door. 'I have a front door and a doorbell, you know.'

'I tried the doorbell but it didn't seem to work. May I come in?'

'That depends on what you want.'

'To help you.'

'I don't need help, thank you. Please peddle your wares elsewhere. You came up a private drive, by the way.'

'The intercom on your gate at the start of it didn't seem to be working either,' the man said, stepping inside the door. 'Or the gate, for that matter.'

That was true, she'd been meaning to get both fixed for ages. She examined the man – slender, well-coiffed in an impeccable suit. 'Tell me what you're selling from there.'

'I'm offering assistance with a problem you have,' he said. His voice sounded quite camp, but the way he seemed to be leering at her she wasn't sure he was gay.

'What's my problem?'

He started walking towards her.

'I don't think I gave you permission,' she called. Nearer his face was intelligent but had a hardness about it.

'Graham Goody said I might be able to help you with a financial problem.'

'Who?'

The man took another step forward. 'Ms Grace, please not let's go through that rigmarole. I gather from Graham you did all that with him. May I come and sit down?'

'You can come another ten yards, but you can't sit down.'

'Far enough?' he said, as he deliberately paced out ten yards.

Grace looked at him up and down. 'So you're a fence.'

'Hardly,' the man said. 'But I think I can help you out of your predicament. I have contacts. Useful contacts. My name is William Simpson.'

'William Simpson – why is that name familiar?'

'I used to be a government adviser some years ago.'

Grace shook her head. 'No, not that. Wait – the police commissioner mentioned your name, I think.'

'Bob Watts? Oh yes, you know him, don't you?'

Grace couldn't figure out the expression on Simpson's face as he said this. A kind of smirk; a kind of look of scorn.

'He's an acquaintance,' Grace said. 'But you know him well?'

'Used to,' Simpson drawled.

Grace didn't like this man at all.

'I believe you have some old money you'd like to renew,' Simpson said.

'I believe Mr Goody believes I have,' Grace said. 'How do you two know each other? Through the SAS?'

'The SAS?' Simpson said.

'Were you in it too?'

Simpson snorted and gestured at his skinny frame. 'Do I *look* like I was in the SAS?' He put his finger to his lip and frowned. 'But, do you know, I don't recall how we met.' Simpson sounding so affectedly bored it made Grace's skin crawl. 'Perhaps it was through Bob Watts.'

'Bob Watts?'

Simpson grimaced. 'Yes, perhaps. But back to the matter in hand. I move money around the world for various clients, big and small. I could do the same for you. For a percentage, of course.'

'So you're not a fence, you're a money launderer,' Grace said.

Simpson gave what he probably imagined to be a charming

smile. 'I think you're forming a bad opinion of me,' he said. 'But I don't do anything illegal. It's like the difference between tax evasion and tax avoidance. One is legal, the other is criminal—'

'Which is which?' Grace interrupted.

Simpson laughed. 'Sometimes I forget, Ms Grace. Listen. I'm a whizz with money and everything I do is above board and within the law – strictly speaking.'

Grace looked down, a small smile on her face. 'I'm not sure how washing stolen money from a robbery can be within the law. Strictly speaking.'

'I don't know anything about money from a robbery,' Simpson said, silky now. 'I simply understood you had some out-of-date money that you needed converting into usable cash, but that you wanted it done anonymously because you're a famous movie star who prefers to shun the limelight these days.

'It's not my job to ask where the money came from – you've been a wealthy woman, I know, and perhaps you simply mistrust banks, so were hoarding it and, because you were so wealthy, forgot about it.'

Grace sat back and saw his eyes flick to her breasts. Suddenly she remembered: he was the father of Bellamy Heap's partner, Kate.

Still didn't mean he wasn't gay, of course, as she knew only too well from the acting world. Every possible permutation of sexuality there, although now the rest of the First World was catching up in that regard. 'As I have already said, the notion that I have this huge stash of old money – accrued in whatever illegal or legal way – is Mr Goody's, not mine.'

'You're still denying you have it?' Simpson sounded exasperated. He spread his hands out, palm up. 'Then it appears I'm wasting my time.'

'And mine. But, since you're here, why don't you stay a little longer?' Grace said. 'Bob Watts is dropping by. I'm sure he'd like to see you again.'

Simpson tried for the charming smile again. Failed again. 'Time presses, Ms Grace.'

Grace remained seated, watching him. When it was clear she was not going to say goodbye in any usual way, Simpson nodded and walked away. He half turned at the garden door. 'Do get in touch if you stumble over a stash of old money, won't you?'

Grace just smiled and gave him a little ta-ta wave. After she heard his car drive away, she took a walk down to her California pine. She sat on the bench there and looked up at the Iron Age earthworks on the top of Plumpton Hill.

When she first fled here, terrified of the sociopathic George Bosanquet, that hill had seemed a looming, threatening presence in what was supposed to be her refuge, her safe haven.

But after the death threats and the failed acid attack by some thug Bosanquet had hired, things eased. She'd always assumed Bosanquet went on to other prey, but she was relieved that, for whatever reason, he never bothered her again.

And then Plumpton Hill became *her* hill. When she was home, which she mostly was, she would walk up there every morning, in all seasons. Her favourite of all was the spring, when the smell of the wild garlic she couldn't help but crush underfoot rose up all around her and all the flowers started to bloom.

She would hate to leave here. Where could she go anyway? But if she did manage to convert this money and hang on to some of it – she was under no illusions about the rapaciousness of Goody and imagined Simpson to be even worse – she probably would need to make herself scarce. Actress though she was, she wasn't a very good liar and she didn't know how she would be if she remained here and remained friendly with Sarah and Bellamy – which she wanted to do – because she feared she would put her foot in it.

She suspected that Goody did have integrity but guessed he was ruthless too. Simpson was something else. She'd had almost a chemical reaction to him, and not in a good way.

EIGHT

Chief Constable Karen Hewitt called Gilchrist and Heap into her huge corner office in the early afternoon. Uptight and corseted, as always, she wasn't happy. She did her best to grimace but Botox had destroyed her grimacing abilities years ago. At least, thought Gilchrist, she hadn't gone for lip-fillers, so didn't have one of those fish pouts. Yet.

'We have to accept,' Hewitt said, tapping a lacquered nail on her desk, '*you* have to accept, that this investigation is fast running into a brick wall. We can't commit more police resources – by which I mean you two, aside from other costs – to this case when finances are so squeezed around here.'

'But we've only just begun,' Gilchrist protested. 'We're waiting for the SOCO report from Elvira's flat. If I could just—'

'If *I* could just almost everything, Sarah,' Hewitt said sternly. 'We have to move on. Look, no one cares about this dead luvvie. Nobody is clamouring for justice. The show must go on.'

Hewitt tried to smirk. Something did happen to her face but Gilchrist couldn't quite figure out what, except that it wasn't the smirk Hewitt was hoping for.

'And it does go on, literally in this case, as performances of the play have now resumed. While in Sussex, county lines drug stuff is taking centre stage, excuse the showbiz reference again.' Again Hewitt's smirk failed. 'Although if you prefer, Sarah, I can put you and DS Heap on finding the cat killer.'

'The cat killer, ma'am?'

'Don't you read your daily briefing? Nine cats have been stabbed to death and seven seriously injured in eight months in Brighton. I'm setting up Operation Diverge to investigate. I can put you in charge if you like.'

'No, thank you, ma'am – with respect.' Gilchrist tilted her head. 'Is that even a crime? Oh – animal cruelty, I suppose.'

'We've been talking to the CPS about that. Animal cruelty only applies if you own the animal. When we catch this person or persons, they believe the best charge to be criminal damage.'

'Criminal damage? On a cat?'

'Animal cruelty is a lesser sentence, that's been their thinking. But first we have to apprehend someone.'

'It'll be some kid,' Gilchrist said.

'Exactly, and since you're going to be investigating kids . . .'

'We are expecting a breakthrough on the theatre murder soon, ma'am.'

'The case I just asked you to put on the back burner, you mean?'

'Ma'am.'

'You know about animal cruelty in kids though, Sarah?'

'That it can escalate to cruelty to humans and ultimately to killing them? That it's one of the tags for a future serial killer? Yes, ma'am, I'm aware.'

'That's right, so this is not an insignificant investigation.' Hewitt shuffled papers for a moment. 'However, if I see your hands are full with the county lines drug situation and that you are getting results with *that* investigation, then I wouldn't want to overburden you by putting this on your plate too.' Hewitt gave what smile she could manage. 'And there is a person of particular interest who is not unknown to you.'

'Ma'am?' Gilchrist said.

'Darren Jones.'

'That little shit.' Gilchrist glanced at Heap, whose lips were pursed. Darren Jones had led a gang of kids, who had sexually assaulted and robbed Kate Simpson.

'Not quite so little now. And it looks like he's one of the main players in getting these kids out into the villages to distribute these drugs. You know we have a major problem in Hassocks with both drugs and knife crime? That seems to be part of his area of control. Or rather, his area of anarchy.'

'I'm aware, ma'am,' Gilchrist said.

'There was a riot there the other week with eight hundred drunken teenagers rampaging around when they all congregated on a silly girl's eighteenth birthday party. She had stupidly posted details on Instagram or WhatsApp or somewhere else public.'

'I'm aware,' Gilchrist repeated.

'He's still underage, isn't he?' Heap said. 'What can we do with him?'

'Arrest him,' Hewitt said. 'Get him in a juvenile offenders unit. He's seventeen and counting so it won't be long now.'

'So shouldn't we wait a few months until he's an adult, ma'am?'

'And let him cause more chaos? Not on my watch, thank you very much. Juvie as soon as.'

'Where he'll recruit more youngsters,' Heap murmured.

'Quite possibly,' Hewitt said. 'Look – without resources we have to accept that we put on plasters and plug gaps. Proactive policing is out of the window for the time being. We have our backs to the wall. We're on the back foot. Whatever cliché you want to use will apply.'

'So we're going after Darren and his scooter gang?' Heap said.

'His scooter gang,' Hewitt said. 'Exactly that. Even without the drug thing they are enough of a pain, if our suspicions are correct, doing snatch and grabs and throwing acid around. Let's run them off the bloody road, shall we?'

'Yes, ma'am,' Gilchrist said, inwardly groaning. How come the person who really couldn't tolerate kids always got stuck with all this kid stuff?

Hewitt steepled her hands. 'There's someone here from the National Crime Agency who is going to give you a briefing and the Agency can provide important logistical support and input.' Hewitt pressed a buzzer on her desk and a moment later a tall, broad-shouldered black guy in a dark brown suit walked in.

'This is John Blackstone from the NCA. As you know, the NCA has responsibility for the nationwide response to county lines drug trafficking. I've asked him to brief you on what's happening and the ways you might synergize with the NCA.'

She held out her hand to Blackstone. 'The room is yours but I will observe, if I may.'

Blackstone shook her hand and smiled at Gilchrist and Heap. 'I don't know how much of this you already know, but let me dive right in.'

Gilchrist gestured to the small conference table and they all sat around it.

'OK,' Blackstone said. 'This trade is worth about £500 million, so there's no limit to what these criminals will do to keep that money coming in. There are some ten thousand kids enslaved in county lines gangs. A lot of them are recruited from pupil referral units – PRUs. The criminals keep an eye on the kids sent to them – it's like hanging a sign round the necks of vulnerable, pliable kids.

'But we're fighting back. A few months ago, in a single week we arrested nearly six hundred people involved in this. We got some £300,000 in cash and forty-six weapons, as well as cocaine, crack cocaine and heroin.'

'I thought they went for the softer drugs,' Heap interjected.

'So did we when we were behind the wave. The other danger is that these kids are vulnerable to all kinds of abuse, including being trafficked for sex slavery. Then you get small gangs taking over a vulnerable person's home for drug dealing.'

'Cuckooing?' Heap said. Gilchrist glanced at him. Trust Bellamy to know the current terminology.

'Exactly that. Now as your chief constable will have told you, we have a National Coordination Centre.'

She's told us bugger all, Gilchrist thought but didn't say.

'We want you both to feed into that and take what information you need out of it. It's hard to keep up with these guys – they're always looking for ways to keep two steps ahead and great intel is the only way to beat them.'

Gilchrist and Heap both nodded. Blackstone touched his tie. 'This thriving ring at work in this city sprawls out over the Downs in every direction. Children as young as seven are brought into it by children of twelve or thirteen, who in turn are handled by kids of sixteen and seventeen.

'They get groomed – given free cannabis, takeaways, clothes, then asked to deliver the odd package to certain addresses. These are the thirteen-year-olds. Usually they are put into bondage by the crooks by being set-up.'

'What do you mean?' Gilchrist said.

'They'll be asked to carry what they are told is a valuable package then they'll get mugged – by the villains themselves, but they won't know that. They're then told they have to pay this *debt* off. There are threats of violence to them or their family. Not to mention sexual exploitation. One poor girl was ordered to go to school in the wrong uniform. The school sent her home without telling her parents and she got pounced on the minute she was out of the school gates. She was raped and forced to perform sex acts.'

Gilchrist shook her head wearily.

'The next step is that they're given a load of cannabis, crack and heroin and so on and told to sell it to other youngsters. The criminals monitor their movements on tracking apps on the phone they're given.'

Blackstone held his hands up palms out. 'We're still behind the tide – the minute we understand it, it changes. The fear and the threat they experience makes these kids – who are victims not criminals, by the way – extremely reluctant to help us.'

'And Darren Jones and his scooter gang are part of this,' Gilchrist said.

'Yes. I know you're onto that. But what we're more interested in, of course, are the adult criminals behind youngsters like Darren Jones; the ones pulling their strings. Do you have any insight into that yet?'

Gilchrist shook her head. 'Not yet.'

Blackstone stood. 'Make that your priority, if you would, Detective Inspector. Don't risk losing the ones at the top to get the easy ones below.' He nodded. 'Thank you for your patience and good luck.' As he left the room he turned. 'Let's keep in touch.'

Hewitt looked at Gilchrist and Heap. 'You're dismissed.'

Bob Watts was in his office watching three seagulls pottering along his windowsill when there was a swift rap on the office door and the sound of it opening. He turned.

'Hello,' he said to the tall Asian woman, smartly dressed in fitted jacket and trousers, standing in the doorway. She was toting a narrow black briefcase. She was maybe in her fifties.

'I'm from the National Crime Agency.'

'Oh, yes. I heard you were visiting to advise the chief constable about county lines drug trafficking.'

'I heard you were in Canada,' the woman said as she advanced into the room to shake his hand.

Watts looked at her sharply. 'Someone published this in the newspapers' – he looked at the name tag on her chest – 'Ms Danvers?'

The woman laughed. She had a pleasant laugh. 'We're the National Crime Agency. We go after organized crime. And that means we're pretty formidable at information gathering.' She gave a little nod. 'Good job in Morocco, by the way, though I understand that some of it is still ongoing. He's a keeper, that Jimmy Tingley.'

Watts moved behind his desk and indicated the chair in front of it. 'I think I want to keep this desk between us – you're scary.'

She laughed again. 'Not scary, just well informed,' she said, taking the seat and neatly crossing her legs. She shrugged. 'Although maybe that comes to the same thing. You want to bring William Simpson down. I don't blame you after what he did to you. But you don't quite know how to do it. Canada didn't work out because the cannabis industry over-extended before it even got started. Ms Lively's way is a good one – we like to follow the money too – but it's not going to give you what you want.'

Watts frowned. 'How the hell can you know what Ms Lively and I discussed?'

Danvers clasped her hands together over her knee. 'Because of her links with William Simpson and his links to unsavoury elements both in our society and abroad, Ms Lively is a person of interest to us.'

Watts frowned. 'So you spy on her. And by extension on us.'

'An affiliate organization does the spying – and most of our work is by extension,' the woman said. She half smiled. 'And we spy only as far as the bedroom door, Commissioner Watts.'

He grimaced and looked away. 'Jesus Christ.'

Danvers gestured at Watts's office and its big picture window with its view of the sea. 'They look after you here but I'm guessing when you're not climbing these walls or counting the seagulls on the windowsill, you're going nuts. Police commissioner – what a Mickey Mouse, politically inspired job that is.

No offence to you. But you're a racehorse pulling a rag-and-bone cart.' She frowned. 'Do they still have rag-and-bone carts anywhere in the UK, I wonder, or am I showing my age?'

'I think they're long gone. You're not in the building to talk about county lines drug trafficking, are you?'

'Me?' She shook her head and re-crossed her legs. 'One of my colleagues is here to deal with that. I'm here to recruit you.' She raised her hand. 'Oh, I know that you don't need to work but I know that, for whatever reason, you feel the need to. Come work for us and you'll have all the tools to do the job properly. Work for us and really make a difference.'

'Work for you?' Watts pointed at the badge on her chest. 'Who are you anyway? I'm guessing Danvers is not your real name.'

She smiled. 'Old habits die hard,' she said softly. 'My background is MI5, MI6, a couple of other security set-ups we don't give a name to. Now I'm a recruiting officer, I guess. For the back room of the agency.'

'Back room? I thought everything was transparent these days in our security forces – and certainly in the National Crime Agency.'

She smiled. 'What's life without a few secrets? Jimmy must have told you that.'

'You keep dropping Jimmy's name. You know him then?'

'Of him, mostly. We sat in a briefing room together once. I've never spoken to the man.'

'What is this job you're offering me?'

'Whatever it is, it has to be better than this one, Bob – may I call you Bob?'

'Since you seem to know all about me, calling me Bob is the least of it. I'm no good at backroom stuff. No good at data mining. I'm old school.'

'You and Tingley demonstrated your old school credentials in Morocco. We have more than enough people doing data mining, thanks, Bob. We want your flair, your leadership qualities and your organizational abilities. We're dealing with big things. Economic crime crossing borders, organized crime, human trafficking, weapon trafficking and drug trafficking – which is how you came onto our radar before your link with

Ms Lively. Cyber crime, of course. I know you have meetings with ROCU, your local regional organized crime unit, so we know you're prepped about our work.'

'And you'll help me bring down William Simpson?'

She shook her head. 'No. You're going to help us do that. He's not a big fish but he's a significant one.'

Watts looked out of the window. He counted the seagulls on the sill. Still three of them. 'Let me think about it.'

NINE

'Bellamy, we have to go up to London again,' Gilchrist said as they went back to their office.

'Would you please tell me why, ma'am? What has this got to do with Darren Jones?'

Gilchrist gave him a look. He didn't flush. 'We've got to find this theatre director. We can't just leave that hanging, despite what the chief constable said.'

'Of course, ma'am. But how?'

'Cat Pinter's parents. This whole thing of them not knowing where she is, I just don't buy it. Do you?'

'Not entirely, ma'am. No.'

'Well then, let's go up there and quiz them a bit harder.'

'Should we clear this with the chief constable?'

'I think we were both at that meeting, Bellamy, so you know the answer.'

'Good.'

'Bellamy? You're not being you.'

'On the contrary, Sarah.'

'Sarah, eh? You're definitely not being you.'

'Maybe this is the real me,' Heap muttered.

Gilchrist and Heap took the train to Clapham Junction and then changed to the Twickenham line. Gilchrist was surprised that she was so disoriented in the bustle at Clapham Junction station, with its couple of dozen platforms and the long walkway connecting them up steep flights of stairs. Maybe she'd been in the country too long but dealing with so many people – yuk.

Cat Pinter's parents lived in a place called Strawberry Hill, one stop further on the Twickenham line as it wound its way to Teddington and Kingston. All Gilchrist knew was that it wasn't part of London, but Bellamy, of course, knew all there was to know.

'Not quite, ma'am,' Heap said. 'But I know about Strawberry

Hill Gothic, which inspired the neo-Gothic revival in the nine-teenth century. Horace Walpole created it in the eighteenth century with his Strawberry Hill house and its interior inspired his *The Castle of Otranto*. I don't know if he ever visited actual Otranto, in Puglia, but he would have done the Grand Tour.'

'Of course he would,' Gilchrist murmured, as they walked from the pretty Strawberry Hill station past smart semi-detached thirties houses with neat front gardens. Sometimes she'd just prefer to have a conversation about something banal – the kind of coffee she liked or pasta – she could talk for a long time about pasta, she thought, touching her stomach. But so often with Bellamy and, for that matter, Bilson, she felt she was the crap one in a *University Challenge* team.

Heap had got Sylvia Wade to phone ahead to the Twickenham police to clear their visit with them and she had arranged the meeting with the Pinters.

They lived on Pope's Grove, right next to the railway line, in a small, semi-detached Georgian villa with, oddly, French windows at the front of the house opening onto the narrow front garden and the road.

'Alexander Pope, the poet and essayist, had a house by the river at the end of the street,' Heap said. 'That's where his famous grotto is, at the end of a tunnel under the main road. Although he did do another grotto down at Marble House in Twickenham. Not as famous though.'

Gilchrist nodded absently as she pressed the bell on the red-painted door. 'Mrs Pinter?' she said as the door was almost immediately opened by a small woman in her forties, maybe early fifties, wearing a very short skirt.

She smiled at them, revealing that she was wearing a brace on her upper set of teeth. Gilchrist had never seen anyone of her age wearing a brace before.

'You're the police from Brighton?' she said. She stood behind the open door. 'Do come in.'

It was a pretty tight fit getting past her without brushing against her. She seemed to enjoy Heap's embarrassment as he edged along the opposite wall to avoid that.

'First door on the right,' Mrs Pinter said.

Gilchrist led the way into a high-ceilinged square reception room with huge double doors separating it from what was presumably the rear reception room on the ground floor. A tall, thin man was standing beside the stripped pine fireplace, his elbow resting on it as if he were posing.

'Tableau vivant,' Heap muttered. Gilchrist had no idea what that meant, but she could tell this would be one of those days when she mostly wouldn't have a clue what Heap was talking about.

'Mr Pinter?' Gilchrist said, stretching out her hand. 'DI Sarah Gilchrist.' She tilted her head towards Heap. 'And this is DS Heap.'

Pinter seemed to be deciding whether to take her hand but after a moment did so. His handshake was limp.

'Detective Inspector.' He nodded at Heap. 'Detective Sergeant. Coffee? Tea?'

'Actually a coffee would be very welcome if it's no trouble,' Gilchrist said. 'Just black.' She looked at Heap, who looked surprised then masked it. 'Detective Sergeant?'

'The same please.'

Gilchrist understood his surprise. They hardly ever accepted hospitality from people they were interviewing. But she'd decided she needed to get a sense of the dynamic between husband and wife. Plus, she actually did fancy a coffee.

Pinter looked at his wife, who was standing by the door, her hands resting on her stomach. 'Lettice?'

She gave an odd little smile and almost a curtsey and left the room. Pinter gestured to the long sofa opposite the fireplace. 'Please – be seated.' He was standing next to a wing chair and Gilchrist expected him to sit too but he remained standing, looking down on them with an affable but slightly supercilious smile on his face.

'You're here to insist on talking about our daughter.'

'She's disappeared, Mr Pinter.'

'Please, call me George.'

'She's disappeared, George,' Heap echoed.

'She's always disappearing is Catherine,' Pinter said. 'No cause for alarm.'

'The alarm isn't that she has disappeared, but that one of the actresses in her latest play has been murdered,' Gilchrist said.

'You're saying our daughter is a suspect?'

'Not in the least, sir,' Heap said. 'We're saying we need to interview her as a witness as part of our investigation.'

'But I understand she wasn't in the theatre at the time of the death so how can she be a witness?' Pinter said.

'A witness in the broadest sense,' Gilchrist said patiently. 'We're trying to build a picture of Elvira Wright's life and recent activities to see if that brings us closer to a motive for her death and the identity of the murderer.'

'I understand,' Pinter said, as his wife came in with a tray of three drinks. She handed one to her husband who put it on the mantelpiece. She placed the tray on a low coffee table in front of Gilchrist and Heap.

'Would you join us, Mrs Pinter?' Gilchrist said. Lettice Pinter glanced at her husband.

'I'd best get on in the kitchen,' she said.

'Please, Mrs Pinter, we need to ask you a few questions about your daughter,' Heap said. He gestured to the wingback chair. 'Please.'

'Lettice,' Mrs Pinter said as she perched on the edge of the chair. 'Mrs Pinter sounds so formal.'

'When was the last time you saw your daughter?' Gilchrist said.

'Two years ago,' George Pinter said.

'She travels a lot?' Heap said.

'I presume,' Pinter said.

'Did you have a falling out?' Gilchrist said. Pinter took a sip of his drink but said nothing. Gilchrist looked at Lettice Pinter. 'Mrs Pinter?'

'Lettice,' she almost whispered.

'Catherine lives a life very different to our way of living,' Pinter said. 'To our ethics.'

'What are your ethics, Mr Pinter?' Heap said.

'Divine law,' Pinter said.

'You're religious, Mr Pinter?' Heap said.

'Are you not, Detective Sergeant?'

'What do you do for a living, Mr Pinter?' Gilchrist said.

'I'm a teacher,' Pinter said. 'At St Catherine's Convent School at the end of the road.'

'Alexander Pope's old house?' Heap said.

'On the site of,' Pinter said.

'You teach Divinity?' Heap said.

'History and English,' Pinter said.

'You have a special subject?'

'I'm a generalist – though I'm rather fond of the poetry of Gerard Manley Hopkins.'

'And Matthew Arnold, I presume,' Heap said.

'Indeed,' Pinter said, tilting his head to examine Heap more closely. 'You know his work?'

'*Dover Beach*, really. You were educated by Jesuits? Stonyhurst College?'

Around now, Gilchrist was realizing she lived a parallel life to her detective sergeant. He was tossing out names of people and places she'd never heard of. *University* flipping *Challenge* again.

'That's correct,' Pinter said.

'Are you religious too, Mrs Pinter?' Heap said.

'Of course,' Pinter said, before his wife could speak – if she was going to speak.

'And your daughter?' Gilchrist said.

Pinter stared at Gilchrist then shook his head. 'It never took with her.'

'Is that the problem?' Heap said.

'There is no problem,' Pinter said.

'You haven't seen your daughter for two years,' Gilchrist said. 'That sounds like a bit of a problem.'

'Have you got children, Detective Inspector?' Gilchrist looked at Mrs Pinter. *Lettice speaks!*

'I don't. But I am a daughter.'

'And you never ignored your parents for a while?' George Pinter said.

'For two years? No.'

'Do you see your daughter's shows?' Heap said.

'No.'

'Never?' Heap said.

'Never,' Pinter said.

'I'm sorry to ask you this question,' Gilchrist said. 'But do you know your daughter's sexuality?'

Lettice Pinter's skirt was high on her thighs. She clasped her hands over her knees and bent forward.

'I don't see how that is pertinent,' George Pinter said, glancing down at his wife's legs.

'I think we have to decide that, Mr Pinter,' Heap said.

'Well, I don't know the answer,' Pinter said.

'Do you know what relationship she had with Elvira Wright, the woman who has been murdered?'

'I've never heard of Elvira and have no idea what their relationship is.'

'Was,' Heap said pointedly. Pinter appeared not to notice.

'Are there any friends of your daughter you can point us to?' Gilchrist said. Pinter shook his head. 'Mrs Pinter?' She looked panicked for a moment then shook her head.

'Was your schism a problem with religion?' Heap repeated.

'There is no schism,' Pinter said.

'And you have no idea where your daughter is?' Gilchrist said.

'No idea,' Pinter said, lifting his chin.

'Can you think of anyone who might have an idea?' Heap said.

'As I said – nobody. We seem to be going round in circles, don't we?'

'Do you work, Mrs Pinter?' Gilchrist said.

Again Lettice Pinter looked panicked.

'She's a homemaker,' Pinter said.

'Why aren't you at school today, Mr Pinter?' Heap said.

Gilchrist was watching Lettice Pinter. She seemed to wilt at the question. Pinter seemed to stand up straighter. 'Sports day,' he said shortly. 'And I knew you were coming.'

'Is there anywhere round here we could get a sandwich?' Heap said abruptly.

'We don't have anything in,' Mrs Pinter said quickly.

'Oh, I wasn't fishing for food from you, Mrs Pinter,' Heap clarified.

'There's the Alexander Pope at the end of the street,' Pinter said. 'They do a range of food.'

Gilchrist and Heap stood. Gilchrist fished in her pocket and came out with a card. She handed it to Pinter. 'We won't take up any more of your time. But if you think of anything . . .'

Out in the street, walking under the railway tunnel as a train shuddered by overhead, Gilchrist said: 'What was all that sandwich lark about?'

'I knew the pub was there. It's across the road from the convent school. I didn't want him wondering why we weren't going back to the station but were heading towards his school.' He smiled shyly. 'Plus, I'm hungry.'

'We're going to his school to check on him?'

'With your permission, ma'am, yes, we are. Didn't you think he was a bit off?'

'Definitely. So we're asking if there is a sports day today? And then taking it from there?'

Heap nodded. The pub was on the right as they reached the end of the street. A big thirties pub with tables out the front but a car park there too. A vaguely Gothic building was across the road with a narrow park beside it and the River Thames beyond. The convent school.

They rang the bell and introduced themselves via the entryphone. The door buzzed and clicked open. To the left as they entered, a smartly dressed woman in her thirties was hovering in an open doorway.

'Can I help?' she said pleasantly.

'We wondered if the headmistress or headmaster was available to speak to,' Gilchrist said.

The woman smiled and shook her head. 'The headmistress isn't here. Can I help? I'm Annabel Culmer, the school secretary.'

'Do you mind us asking where the headmistress is?' Heap said.

'Not at all. It's school sports day.' Culmer saw them exchange glances and frowned. 'Is that why you're here somehow?'

'We're here about George Pinter,' Gilchrist said. 'We understand he has been excused attendance at sports day.'

Culmer looked at them, then gestured to the office behind her. 'Why don't you come in here?'

They followed her into the old-fashioned wood-panelled office. She walked behind her desk and gestured to them to sit at the two chairs in front of the desk.

'Are you from the Twickenham police?'

'Brighton,' Gilchrist said.

Culmer sat down and moved some papers around for a moment. 'I don't understand,' she said. 'Has someone reported him in Brighton?'

'Reported him?' Heap said.

'Oh, dear,' Culmer said, looking anxious. 'Perhaps you need to speak to the headmistress.'

'We're here now,' Gilchrist said. 'What did you mean about reported him?'

Culmer sighed. 'Mr Pinter has been suspended. There have been several serious accusations levelled against him here at the school.'

'And Twickenham police have become involved?'

'No, we're undertaking an internal examination first. But someone has reported him in Brighton?'

'Not so far as I'm aware,' Gilchrist said. 'We're investigating the disappearance of his daughter.'

'Cat?'

'You know her?'

'Of her, really.'

'These accusations, they originate with pupils?' Heap said.

Culmer nodded.

'Sexual abuse?' Heap said.

'Sexual *impropriety*,' Culmer said slowly.

'How long will this internal investigation take?' Gilchrist said.

'You'd need to ask the headmistress that.'

'And is the intention then to take the findings to the police?' Heap said.

'I think that depends on the findings but, again, you would need to ask the headmistress about that.'

When they left the school, Gilchrist gestured across the road to the pub. 'Do you want to get a sandwich?'

'I do, ma'am, but if you're willing to walk a few hundred yards down into Twickenham, there's a lovely pub there right on the river opposite Eel Pie Island.'

'Eel Pie Island – why have I heard of that?'

'Back in the sixties there was a music venue there where the Rolling Stones used to play.'

'And now?'

'A funny warren of wooden houses.'

'You obviously know this area, Bellamy. How come?'

'I lived down here for a few months after school when I wasn't sure what I wanted to do. I was working for an insurance company in Richmond. I used to walk to work along the towpath past Marble Hill House with Ham House on the other side of the river. There's an old-fashioned ferry there for foot passengers. Petersham nurseries is on the other side too.'

'You're my personal guidebook, Bellamy.'

'Always, ma'am.'

They went down a narrow, cobbled street with boutique shops on either side. 'This is like a Lewes lane transported to the Thames,' Gilchrist said. Heap nodded as he led her into the side door of an old waterfront pub. They each ordered a ploughman's and Gilchrist had wine and Heap a half of bitter.

Settled in a quiet corner with a view out onto the sparkling river, Gilchrist said: 'Is it too much of a leap to assume Cat Pinter was abused by her father as a child?'

'It might be. But even if it's true, it doesn't necessarily have anything to do with her disappearance.'

'Necessarily. Nothing more from Pinter's agent?'

'DC Wade phones her every day,' Heap said, making space on the table as their food arrived.

'What about Elvira's agent?'

'The agent who actually took her on has since left the company. Nobody else knew Elvira.'

'Have we been able to talk to the agent who left the company?'

'She's gone travelling and can't be contacted,' Heap said.

'Everybody can be contacted these days, wherever they are.'

'I understand she is trying to find herself so is somewhere up – or maybe it's down – the Amazon with a shamanic community that cuts itself off from the modern world.'

'Well, if she can't find herself, we don't stand much chance of finding her,' Gilchrist said, putting a piece of brie in her mouth. 'Maybe Cat Pinter is with her,' she said through her mouthful of cheese. She never did have any table manners.

Heap chuckled. Gilchrist tilted her head and finished chewing. 'Maybe Cat Pinter *is* with her. Do we know if they were close?'

Heap didn't speak until he had finished chewing. 'Posh bugger,' Gilchrist muttered.

'I'll put Sylvia on it,' he said. 'But remember that time when Stephen Fry was due to open in a Simon Gray play in the West End – no, actually, he did open and did three performances after successful try-outs outside London.'

'Why are you even bothering to ask if I remember?' Gilchrist said, chomping on a piece of celery. 'I don't know anything about theatre. And don't even begin to explain *try-out*.'

'You know enough to know that play you were watching was rubbish,' Heap countered. 'Anyway. Fry got a bad review in the *Financial Times* and ran away. He disappeared for a few days. He just left a note, leaving the production totally in the lurch. Turned up in Belgium and claimed it was stage fright. He never went back to the play.'

'You're suggesting Cat Pinter didn't like the reviews of the play and did a runner because she couldn't cope with her perceived failure. Were the reviews bad?'

'Pretty atrocious and directed mostly at her vision for the play. The pretension of it. Elvira's character was a victim of sexual abuse by her father, wasn't she?'

'I didn't get that,' Gilchrist said, piling pickle and cheddar onto a lump of bread. She glanced at Heap. How come he ate so delicately and she ate like a big galumph?

'One of the reviews said the Zimmer frame the character used was a metaphor for that and how her father had crippled her emotionally.'

'The Zimmer frame said all that?'

'Apparently.'

Gilchrist put down the piece of bread piled high with cheese and chutney – reluctantly. 'So you're linking that to her father's potential abuse of her and that made the play very personal to her which made its rejection a rejection of her own pain and suffering.'

Heap nodded. 'Eloquently put.'

'It was, wasn't it?' Gilchrist said, picking up the open sandwich again. 'Don't ask me where it came from.' She stuffed the open sandwich into her mouth.

'But she's definitely not in Brazil. Or anywhere else outside the UK. Customs have no record of her leaving the country.'

'Do you think she's dead too?' Gilchrist said, when she had finally emptied her mouth.

'Or is Cat the murderer?' Heap said. 'What if she blamed Elvira for the bad reviews, perhaps because she didn't feel Elvira presented Cat's suffering in a suitably worshipful way.'

'But nobody saw her in the theatre that day,' Gilchrist said. 'And certainly not in the rafters.'

'The props girl – Flick somebody? – did say Cat was the only person she'd seen on the gantry.'

'On the night?'

'No. Generally. And a couple were a bit vague.'

Gilchrist looked sharply at Heap. 'I didn't know that.'

'Sorry, ma'am. I just meant they weren't clear when they had last seen Pinter.'

'Two people?'

'Billie Grahame and Bob Thomas.'

'Really?'

'Well, Ms Grahame is a bit doolally as you know, ma'am. I don't think she knows what happens on most days.'

'The large dry martinis and gin and tonics?'

'I wouldn't presume to say, ma'am.'

'But you're a policeman, Bellamy, so you have to presume to deduce.'

'I'm sure the drink is part of it, but many artists don't have brains that work quite like the rest of us, which is perhaps why they are artists and we are not.'

'Oh, we're artists in our way, Bellamy. I agree much of what we do is boringly procedural but the rest requires a little flair.'

'Indeed, ma'am. My parents knew an actress back in Gloucestershire, who was the most unobservant person. Which is odd – you assume actors are very observant – that they would need to be. Anyway, my dad splashed out so Mum could have a big, wide-brimmed black hat for a wedding they were going to. That hat was a big thing in our house and my mum wore it self-consciously but proudly at the wedding and even at the reception.

'I went along too – I was only a kid. My dad and I got separated from my mum briefly at the reception, but we saw her talking to the actress for a while then pointing over at us. The actress came over to us and chatted, rather stiltedly. I couldn't think of anything to say but thought I should try, so said, "What do you think of mum's hat?" "What hat?" the actress said. "Is she wearing one?"'

Gilchrist laughed, then looked fondly at Heap. 'I've never heard you talk about your family before.'

Heap flushed. 'Sorry.'

'No, no – don't be.' She smiled. 'I'm flattered that you shared that with me.'

'I've been thinking about my family a lot lately.'

'Really?'

'A family history project in my spare time.'

'You have spare time? I thought you worked all the time when you weren't spending it with Kate.'

'Kate's away on her writing course for a couple of weeks.'

'Yes, I know. Everything OK there?'

Heap shrugged. 'Sure. But it means I've got a bit of time.'

'That deductive mind gets restless.'

'Something like that, ma'am.'

She pushed her plate away. 'We should get going.'

'Back to Sussex?'

'I guess. How do you feel about calling round on Mrs Jones and Darren?'

'Sure,' he said. 'He does still live at home.'

'Most of these young gangsters do. So how do we take down the scooter gangs, Bellamy? I have to admit I have no ideas or any clue how to approach this. Because they are underage, I feel I'm treading on eggshells, when my strong urge is to give these feral kids a good hiding.'

'You've had worse ideas, ma'am.'

'Oh, really – when?'

Heap flushed. 'That's just a figure of speech, ma'am.'

'What exactly *is* a figure of speech, Bellamy? Some kind of shape?'

'Perhaps another time, ma'am?'

'Bellamy, you're my fount of all knowledge – don't dry up on me now.'

'*Font*,' Heap said quietly.

'Hang on, I'm sure you've told me before it was fount not found and now you're saying it's *font*? What's the difference, anyway? No, don't bother to tell me – I'm sure you've told me that before too.'

On the train back down to Brighton, Gilchrist managed to stay awake, which was a first, and watch the countryside go by, while Heap tapped away on his iPad.

She'd wanted to be working back in Brighton catching real criminals. And now she'd got her wish but with bloody teenagers.

A couple of years ago she and Heap had got stuck doing inter-agency work about youth gangs in Brighton and Hove. Actually, Bellamy, responsible copper and eager beaver that he was, hadn't seen it as 'getting stuck'. He'd seen it as important work. Which it was, of course. But she'd always hankered for the bigger stuff, the grown-up crime, breaking-up the crime families and coming down hard on career criminals.

Now, the youth gangs *were* the career criminals and most were closely involved with the epidemic of county lines drug trafficking, employing kids even younger than themselves.

Darren Jones was a thug who had been involved with the inquiry into the Save Salthaven Lido killings and who had led a gang of young teenagers in assaulting Kate Simpson in Woodvale cemetery.

He'd got a token slap on the wrist for that assault and now he was riding round on a brand new Vespa scooter, with all the bells and whistles, all over Brighton. He could afford it – or he'd been given it – because Intel said he was managing a couple of dozen twelve-year-olds who were distributing drugs via the train lines out of Brighton, along the coast and up over the Downs. Proving that was something else again, of course.

TEN

Jimmy Tingley was sitting outside a café on Rue St Catherine in Montreal drinking a *biere bleu* from the bottle – when in Rome and all that. He was watching the world go by. He'd come to Canada on a whim, even though he had no work to do here.

But what the hell else was he going to do? He thought of places he'd been or rather been grounded in and decided this was as good a place as any. Actually, that wasn't even it – the fugitive thought that clarified for a moment what his life was about. Ha! What his life was about implied a grand purpose. His life, like anybody else's, a string of accidents, purposes gone awry, things imposed.

He'd always been embarrassed to quote a pop singer – John Lennon – about life is what happens when you're making other plans. He agreed with Noel Coward about the potency of popular songs but hated their sentimentality, cheap emotion and, usually, bad writing. But it was even worse when he discovered that Lennon had got that quote about life from an astrologer from the *Daily Mail*.

The bartender brought another beer just as Tingley's phone rang. He didn't recognize the number. One of the Henfield retired SAS gang?

'Hello?' he said warily.

'Jimmy Tingley,' a pleasant woman's voice said. 'So nice to connect with you.'

'Who's speaking and how did you get this number?'

'Questions, questions, Mr Tingley. My name is Danvers. I work for the National Crime Agency in the UK. I have a proposition for you.'

At Darren Jones's ex-council house, Gilchrist and Heap observed two fancy Vespas parked outside and an extension to the house over the garage.

'That's indicative,' Heap said. Gilchrist nodded, just as DC Sylvia Wade phoned her. Gilchrist put it on speaker.

'Something urgent, ma'am, but can I just quickly say on the theatre murder case: SOCO has nothing of use to report from Elvira's flat. No interesting DNA – it's as if nobody else but her had ever been in the flat, which is unusual.'

'Wiped?'

'Well, her DNA was there so they don't see how other DNA could have been wiped. And there was no handy diary or letters. She genuinely didn't seem to have any friends or family.'

'OK, thanks Sylvia. And the urgent thing?'

'It's the scooter gangs, ma'am,' Wade said. 'Last night.'

'What?'

'A stabbing,' Wade said.

'Fatal?'

'It remains to be seen, ma'am,' Wade said.

'Who is the victim?' Gilchrist said.

'Darren Jones,' Wade said.

Gilchrist grimaced. 'Where is he?'

'Royal Sussex. Intensive care.'

'I assume we're there.'

'Yes, ma'am.'

'His mother?'

'Yes, ma'am.'

'CCTV?'

'I'm on that.'

'Witnesses?'

'Ditto.'

'Thanks, Sylvia. Hang on.' Gilchrist turned to Heap and said quietly, '*Ditto* me this, Bellamy – was this a turf war do you think?'

'Either that or he hadn't delivered the goods for the bigger boys pulling his strings.'

Gilchrist raised her voice. 'Sylvia – how much Intel do we actually have on how these gangs are structured around here?'

'You mean names and faces, ma'am? Not so much. We don't know who most of the little kids doing the running around are. We know a number of Darren-level boys in the different gangs. We don't have very much at all on who they're working for – and then there's probably another level above that.'

'Sylvia, get on to the NCA and see if they have any updates they haven't shared with us yet.'

Parking around the Royal Sussex Hospital was always a nightmare, so they pulled rank and parked on double yellows where it wasn't going to be *too* disruptive. They had about a five-minute walk once they were in the huge hospital to find the intensive care unit.

Two policemen stood guard on a small ward. 'Any trouble?' Gilchrist said when she'd identified herself and Bellamy.

'Aside from the mother you mean, ma'am?' said the beefier of the two, a PC McGregor.

'She's in there?' Gilchrist said, gesturing with her chin at the ward behind them.

'It's unusual that you can't hear her now,' McGregor said.

'Well, she is his mother and he has been stabbed,' Heap said equably.

'It's not that, sir. She's really angry with him for being such an idiot as to get knifed.'

'Again, it's not unusual for a mother to get angry that someone they care about has been careless,' Heap said.

The two constables exchanged glances. The second one, PC Howe, spoke up. 'We don't think she realizes she can be heard out here. Although there are four beds in there, there is nobody else in the room. Plus, she's drunk, so doesn't know how loud she is being.'

'Go on, Constable,' Heap said.

Howe glanced at McGregor, who nodded encouragement to him. 'We think she might be implicated in whatever he's involved in.'

'In fact, we wonder if he might be working for her.'

Blustery, vulgar Mrs Jones a criminal kingpin? Gilchrist couldn't see it somehow. She seemed to be thick as two short planks. And if that were an act and she was a cunning crime boss, would she be shouting stuff that might implicate her? Gilchrist couldn't see it.

'Very good, Constables,' she said now. 'Thank you for being so alert. We're going to talk to her now.'

'Mrs Jones,' Heap said as they reached the bed. 'How is Darren?'

'Much you care,' she muttered without turning round to look at them. She was sitting hunched forward looking down on her son and stroking his face. His eyes were closed and Gilchrist couldn't decide if his always pale face was whiter than usual or not.

Other than the various tubes sticking out of him, he didn't look much different to the last time she'd seen him. Still the same vicious, ferret-faced boy. Although the stubble was something new. Gilchrist resisted the urge to ask his mother when he had started shaving – or in this case not shaving.

She knew she should but she felt no sympathy for Darren Jones at all. As best she knew, he'd spread misery wherever he went. He was malicious and bullying and cruel. Plus, he'd led an assault on her friend Kate and got away with a slap on the wrist.

She glanced at Heap. He was working the muscles in his jaw as he looked down at Darren. 'Did this happen when he was out yesterday evening, Mrs Jones?' Heap asked.

'Leave me alone,' Mrs Jones said. 'Can't you see I'm grieving?'

'Would it be better if we took you down to the station and interviewed you more formally?' Heap said. 'Because we could.'

Mrs Jones turned then. 'Oh God, it's you two fuckers.'

Gilchrist ignored that. 'We understand from the hospital that Darren is going to recover. So there is no need for grieving. What do you know about what happened to him?'

'I don't know nothing,' Mrs Jones said, looking Gilchrist up and down. 'You've put on weight, in't ya?'

That one hit home. 'We've heard a rumour that he works for you,' Gilchrist said tersely.

'Are you kidding?' She scowled – and it was quite a scowl. 'He don't lift a finger for me. He wouldn't know a tea towel if I hit him in the face with it, which many a time I've been tempted to do.'

Gilchrist shook her head wearily. God, she wanted to punch this woman.

'We didn't mean that kind of work,' Heap said, catching Gilchrist's expression. 'The work that means he can afford two brand new scooters.'

'Oh they're not his. He's been lent them for work. For making deliveries.'

'Who lent them?'

'Why you asking that when he's on death's door?'

'He's out of danger, Mrs Jones,' Gilchrist said. 'And we're trying to find out who did this to him.'

'Well, it's obvious, in't it? Some other kid from one of the streets nearby, nicking his scooter.'

'His scooter has been stolen?'

'I assume so. He didn't come home on it anyway.'

'So, who owns the two scooters outside your house?' Heap said.

'There's always scooters outside the house – people coming and going. I can't keep track.'

'What happened when he did come home?' Gilchrist said.

'He rang the bell and when I answered it he fell into the hallway covered in blood. So I called the ambulance and I must say they were quick.'

'Did he tell you who'd done it?'

'He didn't tell me anything.' She looked down at her son. 'And look at him now.'

'The business he's in—' Heap began.

'Deliveries.'

'Mrs Jones, we have reason to suspect that he's delivering drugs for drug syndicates,' Gilchrist said. 'I'm sure you've heard of county lines drug trafficking.'

'What makes you think that?'

'Mrs Jones, I don't have time to give you the list. Do you know if there is an older man or men he habitually sees?'

'What's that *habity* word mean?'

'Often,' Heap said.

'No.'

'What do you do for a living, Mrs Jones?'

'I'm a homemaker.'

'You're on benefits?'

'So?'

'And that's your only source of income?' Heap said.

'That's right. I scrape by.'

'That looks like a new extension on top of your garage – extra bedroom, is it?' Heap said.

'It's a small house. We was bursting out of it.'

'How did you pay for it?' Heap said.

'A loan, if it's any of your business.'

'You got a loan when you're on benefits? From a bank or a building society?'

'A private loan. Look, is this the right time to have this conversation, do you think?'

'Not a payday loan?'

'No – a private one, from someone I know. Did you hear what I said?'

'High interest?' Gilchrist said.

'What business is that of yours, when my Darren's lying here? You should concentrate on catching who did this to him.' Jones turned her attention to her son, squeezing his hand.

'That's what we're trying to do,' Gilchrist said. 'How are your repayments made? In cash? Mrs Jones?'

'Cash, yes, every week,' Jones said, still focused on her son.

'How can you afford that?' Heap said.

'Interest only for now,' Jones said grudgingly.

'Are you renting the extension out?' Heap said.

''Course not. That would affect my benefits.'

'Mrs Jones, we're not looking to report you for cheating on your benefits, if you are,' Heap said. 'We're interested in getting the bad person who did this to Darren. That's all we're interested in.'

Jones turned, her face angry. 'That's what you said last time about him helping you identify those poofs in the cemetery and next thing you know he's in court about something else and never got no reward as you promised. Why should I believe a bloody word either of you say?'

'Well, that was a bit more complicated,' Gilchrist said. 'Your son had broken a criminal law. If you have somehow fiddled your benefits, that is a civil matter.'

'I haven't fiddled my fucking benefits.'

'Can we speak to your lodger, Mrs Jones?' Heap said.

'You seem to be able to do whatever you want.'

'What is this person's name?'

'Clive Pyne.'

'Friend of yours?'

'So?'

'Do you have a number for him?' Heap said, gesturing at the mobile phone on the table by the hospital bed.

'Is he the man who made the loan to you?' Gilchrist asked.

'I don't have to answer that,' Jones said.

I think you just have, Gilchrist thought.

'Is Mr Pyne at your home now?' Heap said.

'I have no idea. I'm not his bloody keeper.'

'How long has he been lodging with you?' Heap said.

'Listen, are you going to find out who stabbed my boy?'

'When you give us some names to go on, of course we are,' Gilchrist said. 'In the meantime, if you could give us Mr Pyne's number we can leave you alone and continue our investigations.'

Reluctantly, Jones fumbled with her phone and read out the number. They thanked her and excused themselves.

'Keep earwigging, gentlemen,' Heap said as they passed the two constables on guard outside.

'Sir,' McGregor said to Heap's back.

'What do you think, Bellamy?' Gilchrist said when they were back in the car.

'Probably the same as you, ma'am.'

'Which is?'

'Shall we go to Mrs Jones's house to interview Pyne?'

'Let's talk to him on the phone first. And, right now, let's redeploy in a caff. Any preference?'

At Heap's suggestion they went to the café on the mezzanine balcony overlooking the main collection in the Pavilion Museum and Art Gallery. Gilchrist looked down on the Arts and Crafts furniture – Bilson had told her once that's what it was – and the surrealist art (ditto) on the wall. 'They haven't put that painting back that got nicked when all the black magic stuff was going on a couple of years ago,' she said.

'They can't think that nonsense is going to happen again, can they?' Heap said, sipping his mint tea.

Gilchrist took a slug of her long black. 'The lodger is next up the chain?' she said.

'Quite possibly. That's a regular pattern.'

'And the loan from him for the extension is hanging over their heads and they're accruing massive interest, so they have to do what he wants.'

'Again, a regular pattern. Threats of violence, sexual and otherwise.'

'Probably,' Gilchrist agreed. 'I know it sounds bitchy, but Mrs Jones is probably having sex with him without needing to be coerced. Or not at first anyway.'

'That is bitchy, ma'am, if you'll forgive me. If she is having sex against her wishes now, then we need to protect her.'

'You're right, of course. Bellamy my conscience.'

Heap lifted his phone. 'Shall I ring him?'

Gilchrist looked around. There was nobody near them. 'Sure. But I'm going to phone Sylvia for a catch-up.'

When they had both concluded their conversations, Gilchrist said: 'And?'

'An hour from now in the Cricketers,' Heap said.

'Excellent. Jimmy Tingley's old haunt. I haven't been there for an age. Do we know where Jimmy is, by the way?'

'He's more the friend of Bob Watts and you, ma'am, than me. I have no idea where he is.'

'I must ask Bob.'

'Do we have need of him?' Heap said.

'We always have need of him.'

'Rule of law, ma'am.'

'Says the man who beat up a fellow police officer because rule of law wasn't going to work with him.'

Unusually, Heap didn't flush. 'What did DC Wade have to report?'

'Nothing. We seem to be wading through treacle.'

'But inching forward, nevertheless. Here's what I think, ma'am. It's a bit left field.'

'Not like you to be left field – not that I'm really sure what that means, but I'm guessing.'

'I think Clive Pyne should be considered as the person who stabbed Darren.'

Gilchrist tilted her head. 'Go on.'

'I'm certainly not making presumptions and suggesting we narrow the focus of our investigation but I can see the model, as I'm sure you can. Darren stuck doing this stuff for his mum's lodger. Doesn't deliver the goods or, more probably, knowing Darren, tries to be a smartarse and rip Pyne off. But Pyne is expecting that. So he knifes Darren.'

'OK. Interesting hypothesis. But why would Pyne hang around?'

'Because he knows neither Darren nor his mum are going to hand him over. He feels safe. Or arrogant.'

'The latter, probably,' Gilchrist said, disliking Pyne already.

'Well, we could be at the start of a chain here,' Heap said. 'Which is good.'

ELEVEN

Nimue Grace stood at her kitchen sink, thinking furiously. She knew the clichés about actresses and, for that matter, redheads, but that had sometimes worked in her favour. She was brighter than people assumed, dazzled as they were by her looks – well, used to be dazzled back in the day.

But what to do about Goody? She went and looked for her phone book. Most of her friends stored numbers and addresses on their mobile phones but she was old school, not least because she was prone to losing her phones and was useless at backing them up. She flipped through to the Bs and then the Ws – she was not entirely consistent in whether she listed somebody by their first or last names – until she found the phone number for Bob Watts.

She didn't know where in the world he was, but she thought it was time she found out a bit more about Goody.

The Cricketers was an old-style Victorian pub at the edge of the Lanes. Its original open, cobbled courtyard was now roofed in, which made it an attractive place to hang out in summer and winter. Not much of a view, though the passers-by in Brighton were always worth watching.

Gilchrist knew it had been Jimmy Tingley's favourite pub for years. Sitting there with his rum and pep and his cigarette packet and lighter carefully aligned. Gilchrist genuinely liked Tingley and wondered where he was and if he was OK.

She led Heap into the covered courtyard and they sat at a table with a view of the street in front of them. They didn't know what Pyne looked like, but he'd said he would find them. And he did.

'Don't get up,' a stocky man in jeans and denim jacket said, as he put his pint on the table and sat down opposite them.

'Mr Pyne?' Heap said.

Clive Pyne nodded.

'Thanks for agreeing to see us,' Gilchrist said.

Pyne smiled. It was an odd smile because at some point he had been the victim of an acid attack and his face had that smooth shiny look and puckering of the skin graft patient, especially around the right-hand side of the mouth and underneath the right eye.

Gilchrist could tell that he was looking for a reaction to his face. She wasn't going to give it. She kept her face neutral and wondered who had done it to him. And it seemed to increase the likelihood that he was involved in some bad stuff.

'What happened to your face?' Heap said, unusually directly for him.

'Have a guess,' Pyne said, approximating a smirk.

'Acid attack. A business rival.'

'Business rival? You're making assumptions, aren't you?'

'Just unfortunate timing, then?'

'They wanted my scooter,' Pyne said, and took a long drink of his beer.

'You ride a scooter, Mr Pyne?' Heap said.

'Easiest way to get around in traffic.'

'Is that your scooter parked outside the Jones household?'

'What's the registration?'

Heap told him.

'That's mine, yeah.'

'And the other one?' Heap read off the registration.

'Yep, that's mine too. Bit of a Mod, truth be told – a bit late in the day, I admit, but we all have our foibles, don't we?'

'So neither of them are Darren's?' Heap said.

'Well, I let him use them, obviously, as I'm their lodger.'

'What do you get in return?' Gilchrist said.

Pyne looked at her. 'I don't get what you're asking.'

'I'm just wondering why you are lodging with them at all and what you get out of lodging with them.'

Pyne frowned – he could do that, at least. 'Well I'm lodging with them because I need somewhere to live and I get a roof over my head. That suit you?'

'What do you do for a living, Mr Pyne?' Heap asked.

'This and that. Nothing regular.'

'So who threw the acid in your face?' Gilchrist said.

'I told you. Somebody who wanted my scooter.'

'Well, at least they managed not to splash any on the scooter,' Heap said. 'That must have been a relief.'

Pyne touched his distorted face. 'It's not something that's uppermost in my mind.'

'When did it happen?' Gilchrist said.

'A couple of years ago. Why?'

'Are you still having treatment?' Gilchrist asked.

Pyne shook his head. 'It is what it is.' He touched his face again. 'This is me now.'

'I suppose it's the modern equivalent of the razor gangs on the racetrack back in the thirties,' Heap said conversationally. 'You know, the rival gangs clashing and using open razors to slash each other on the face. Remember Richard Attenborough in the film of *Brighton Rock*?'

'You're an erudite bloke, aren't you?' Pyne said.

'Erudite,' Heap said. 'Not a word you hear every day.'

'What, you mean from people like me?' Pyne said, a sneer in his voice.

'I don't know what kind of person you are. Unless you mean crooked people.'

Gilchrist glanced at Heap. He was going in a bit strong, wasn't he?

Pyne did his lopsided smile and leaned towards Heap. 'You have a charge to make against me?'

'All in good time,' Heap said. 'Did Darren throw the acid at you?'

What the f—? Gilchrist looked more intently at Heap. Where did that come from? Then she looked at Pyne. Although it was hard to read his damaged face she saw the surprise and then the furious thinking going on.

'Mrs Jones told me,' Heap said. Which, as far as Gilchrist knew, was a lie.

'Did she?' Pyne said slowly. 'Did she?'

'She told me everything, actually,' Heap said. 'And I promised we'd protect her in return.'

'Did you?' Pyne said.

'And we will,' Heap said quietly.

'So Big Brain – what's your hypothesis? Yes, I read books. I know posh words like *erudite* and *hypothesis*.'

'Good for you,' Heap said. 'Nothing like a good book.'

Pyne sat back and took another glug of his beer.

'Look, if you help us roll this up, we can help you,' Heap said.

'Roll this up?' Pyne laughed. 'You can't roll this up. You don't have the capability or the resources. Best thing you can do is just step aside. There's a tsunami coming and it's best to get out of its way.'

'What do you mean?' Gilchrist said.

'Look around. People want drugs. The only sensible thing to do is legalize them. But sensible is the last thing that the British government is. So they sit on their high horses and pontificate and waste millions on drug control, which ain't gonna work, of course. And there is this massive amount of drugs flooding into the country. That can't be stopped.'

'We can stem it,' Gilchrist said.

Pyne looked at her. 'Ms Canute, you look more intelligent than somebody who would make that asinine statement. It's unstoppable.'

'Nothing is unstoppable if you have the will,' Heap said.

'Ayn Rand fan, are you, Detective Sergeant? Or another Canute?'

'You *are* an educated man,' Heap said. 'It's usually Cnut these days though. And no, I'm not. Either thing. I believe in good triumphing over evil.'

'Religious then,' Pyne said.

Heap shook his head. 'Not that either. Humanist. I believe in the human spirit.'

Pyne leaned back and laughed. He had a surprisingly melodious laugh. 'Then you're truly fucked.' He leaned forward again. 'But listen, I had no idea I was coming to have such a stimulating conversation with two plods. Thank you. Really.' He started to rise.

'Where do you think you're going?' Gilchrist said. 'We haven't finished with you.'

Pyne looked down on her. 'I'm not aware I'm under arrest.

I did you the courtesy of coming down here to talk with you. Do me the courtesy of allowing me to leave.'

'Darren threw the acid at you and now you've made him your slave,' Heap said.

Pyne looked down on Heap then slowly sat down again and took another drink from his pint. 'His mother told you that?'

Heap didn't reply. Instead he continued. 'So now he has to do your bidding and so does his mum.'

'You're talking about his mum servicing me sexually. Well, yes and no. Yes, she is, but no, it's not coercive. Very healthy woman, that Mrs Jones. I would say it's almost the other way round. She's using me to stay healthy.'

'And Darren?'

'What – you mean sex? Not me, mate, I'm not into kiddy fiddling or boy-on-boy stuff. Just call me old-fashioned.'

'I meant, is his mum why he threw the acid in your face?' Heap said. 'Because he didn't approve?'

Pyne shrugged. 'Something like that. Teenagers – what you gonna do?'

'But you say you suffered an acid attack a couple of years ago. Why wait so long to stab him.'

'Assuming I did stab him.' He took another drink. 'Well, I know revenge is meant to be a dish eaten cold, but I've forgiven him for the acid attack. Sort of.'

'Why stab him then? Allegedly?'

'Would you say Darren is a kid you could put your trust in? No, me neither. He's a devious delinquent who's always trying it on. If I were to have stabbed him, I expect it would be because he was trying to rip me off but was too stupid to do it without it being obvious.'

'So he does do deliveries for you,' Heap said. 'Didn't he deliver what he was supposed to?'

Pyne sat back again. 'You're not going to let this go, are you?'

'Not a chance,' Gilchrist said. 'We have enough information from the NCA to put you away tomorrow. Help us nail your bosses. It's your only way out.'

'My bosses?' Pyne said. 'You'd never get anywhere near my bosses.'

'We can get you though,' Gilchrist said.

'I don't think you understand how the justice system works if you think you could put me away tomorrow, miss.'

'Detective Inspector. Did you stab Darren?'

'You're moving right along, aren't you?' Pyne drained his glass. 'I'm getting another. Same again for you two?'

'We're fine,' Gilchrist said.

'If you want my help, you've got to understand pub etiquette,' Pyne said.

'Same again would be very nice,' Heap said. Pyne rested his hand on Heap's shoulder as he walked by.

Gilchrist twisted to watch him go. 'You think he's coming back?'

Heap shrugged. 'Seventy–thirty. But where is he going to go?'

'Could this be a way forward?' Gilchrist said.

'Maybe,' Heap said. 'But you're doing a big bluff with the NCA stuff.'

'You can talk!' Gilchrist said, draining her glass. 'Who do you think his bosses are?'

'Well, the big Brighton gangs are pretty much gone now so I guess we're looking at Albanians.'

'Why does that thought fill me with dread?' Gilchrist said.

'Because you know how ruthless and heartless Albanian gangsters are?'

'That would be it.' Gilchrist tilted her head as Pyne returned, holding the three drinks in hands that she only now noticed were huge. Pyne saw her looking.

'Yeah, I'm reverse Donald Trump.' He gave Gilchrist's breasts a quick once-over. 'You should bear that in mind.'

'In your dreams,' she muttered as he sat down.

'Cheers,' Pyne said, pointing his raised glass in their general direction. 'So where were we?'

'You were about to spill the beans about your Albanian bosses,' Heap said, raising his glass.

'You *are* a clever bugger, aren't you?' Pyne said to Heap. 'You tricked me earlier but you won't do that again. You're going to come up a bit short with regards to evidence against me. Besides which you haven't formally cautioned me so this entire conversation is inadmissible were you to try to use it against me further down the line.'

'We're not trying to trick you, Mr Pyne,' Gilchrist said. 'But, I'll be honest, we do need your help.'

'Tell me something I don't know. And what do I get in return? Immunity? A reward? Darren told me about you two – how you stiffed him on a reward.'

'That was more complicated,' Gilchrist said. 'He'd done something really shitty he had to pay for.' She tilted her head. 'Now shall we get on?'

'I'm glad you don't think allegedly stabbing a little shit is shitty.' Pyne did his tortured smile. 'At your disposal, Detective Inspector.'

'Who do you work for?'

'Well, that comes under the heading of privileged information.'

'Because?' Heap said.

'Because they'll kill me if I tell you. Without any hesitation. And then they'll kill you two. And your pets.'

'We can look out for ourselves, thank you, Mr Pyne,' Gilchrist said.

Pyne glanced at Heap. 'What, this squirt?'

Heap just smiled. Gilchrist said quietly: 'Don't you worry about DS Heap. And he doesn't have any pets. Now tell us about your bosses.'

'Immunity? Reward?'

'Depends how deep in you are,' Heap said. 'Maybe a reduced sentence.'

'No way I'm going to prison.'

'No way you're not,' Heap said. 'If only for the *alleged* stabbing.'

'For at least a token time, you mean?' Pyne said.

Neither Heap nor Gilchrist answered. Pyne looked away. 'Look, I'm just a small cog,' he said after a moment.

'Look, we're going to see what we can do,' Gilchrist said. 'OK? But you stabbed a kid and you're involved in exploiting other kids in a very scummy business.'

Pyne looked down at the table and didn't say anything. 'I'm not proud of myself,' he finally said. He picked up his drink. 'And Darren isn't a minor.'

'He's seventeen,' Heap said.

Pyne sighed. 'He swore to me he was eighteen. But I guess that's irrelevant in the scale of things.'

'Just spill,' Gilchrist said. 'Is your boss Albanian?'

'Bosses. Yes. You don't know what you're taking on here. The barbarians aren't just at the gate, they're inside the gate and burning down the city.'

'It's not that long ago we had to deal with some "barbarians" from another part of the Balkans,' Gilchrist said. 'They were about as brutal as you can possibly imagine. We managed.'

Heap looked at Gilchrist. She realized why. The attempted Balkan takeover of Brighton crime was before his time, back in the day when the local crime boss had been dubbed the Last King of Brighton.

'Where do we find your bosses?' Heap said.

'I deal with only one, but he is one of many.'

'We'll take them one by one,' Gilchrist said. 'A name, please.'

'Kobel.'

'Where is he?'

'Not far away,' Pyne said. 'Over the Downs. Plumpton Manor. Do you know it?'

Gilchrist and Heap exchanged glances. 'Oh, yes.' Gilchrist nodded. 'We know it.'

'What is Liesl Rabbitt up to?' Gilchrist said to Heap after Pyne had left. Rabbitt was the Greek-Albanian widow of 'Major' Richard Rabbitt. He had recently been killed at Grace's lake. Liesl seemed to have inherited his big house – Plumpton Manor – even though they were separated at the time of his murder.

They had met one of Liesl's Albanian friends, as hard-faced as Liesl herself. 'Is her friend, the gangster's moll, living there with her? Is she Kobel's woman, do you think?'

'They are the obvious link with Albanian drug gangsters, though I understood the Albanians to be focusing solely on class A drugs, not on marijuana.'

'Not any longer it seems. They follow the money.' She looked at her watch. 'Let's call it a night, shall we? It's been a long day and I have to go back over the Downs.'

'Are we taking tomorrow off, ma'am?'

'Well, it is a Sunday, Bellamy.'

'Rust never sleeps, ma'am.'

'There's something I have to do,' she said. 'But let's talk later in the day.'

TWELVE

At Sunday lunchtime Sarah Gilchrist and Mark Harrison, the ostrich farmer, were in the Jolly Sportsman in Plumpton.

'Have you heard, Sarah?' he said, draining his cider and signalling the passing waitress for another.

'Heard what?' she said, as she tucked into a Sunday roast with all the trimmings.

'They found this huge thigh bone in a cave in the Crimea.'

Gilchrist looked at him and said through a mouthful of Yorkshire pudding: 'You're not mixing me up with Bellamy, are you? Why would I be interested in that?'

Harrison laughed. 'I thought you said you were embarrassed to be so ignorant and wanted to know more.'

'I'm not sure I put it quite like that but I'm not sure a thigh bone in a Crimean cave was included in my thirst for knowledge.' Harrison smiled fondly at her and winked. 'Oh, wait,' she said. 'I should have guessed – it's a giant ostrich bone.'

He laughed. 'This bird dwarfs my ostriches or any modern flightless bird. It weighed half a tonne and was three and a half metres tall – that's eleven and a half feet in old money – and the find means it was roaming around Europe when the first humans got here from Africa. The bone is between 1.5 and 1.8 million years old.'

'Were there some kind of humans in Europe then?'

'They got to Europe about 1.2 million years ago, but this bird was still roving about. You know there was a bird around the same size in the rainforests of Australia's Northern Territory from about fifteen million years ago to just 50,000 years ago. The Demon Duck of Doom.'

Gilchrist spluttered her wine and had a brief coughing fit. 'The Demon Duck of Doom?'

Harrison laughed. 'Catchy, isn't it? Some researcher had an

eye for a headline. Real name Bullockornis something-or-other. But it had a head the size of an entire horse and a razor-sharp beak, so you didn't want it taking a swipe at you.'

'Absolutely.' She took another sip of her wine. 'Actually, that was quite interesting.'

Harrison put his fork down. 'I was only telling you because I like your company and I was trying to prolong what I'm pretty certain is going to be our last intimate get-together. This morning was a very fond farewell, by the way. Thank you.'

'What are you talking about?' Gilchrist said, glancing at Harrison and away.

'Who is Bob?'

Gilchrist reached for her wine but didn't pick it up. 'Why do you ask?'

'Wonderful Sarah Gilchrist, you talk in your sleep. Oh, don't worry, you don't say anything coherent—'

'When do I ever?'

'—but last night you said the name Bob. I mean it's not like you said his name when we were . . . you know . . . and if your dreams aren't private, then what is? So no reason at all for you to tell me.'

Gilchrist sat back and gently pushed her plate away. She took a glug of her wine. She never remembered her dreams. Never ever. She looked around the pub, astounded to hear she'd said Bob Watts's name. And, as if thought of the name summoned him, like some kind of genie, there Watts was, walking to a table at the other end of the pub, Nimue Grace in tow.

'What's happening with Liesl Rabbitt these days?' Gilchrist said abruptly.

'Haven't a clue. Never see her. She got rid of the llamas, that's about all I know.'

'You haven't bumped into a bloke called Kobel, have you?'

Harrison frowned and shook his head. 'Not that I'm aware of.'

Gilchrist went quiet.

'I don't mind what you say,' Mark Harrison said, leaning into her and talking quietly into her ear. 'You've got so much work on, the timing isn't right, it's you not me. But please,

please, don't say: "how many ostrich egg omelettes can one woman eat?"'

Gilchrist dragged her eyes away from Bob Watts and Nimue Grace and looked at Harrison, giving his hand a squeeze. 'I wouldn't be so crass.' She held his look for just a moment then dropped her eyes.

'So no Canada for you after all,' Grace said as the waitress poured her Prosecco.

'I missed the boat on that one.'

Grace raised her glass. 'Cheers.' She looked beyond him. 'That's odd.'

Watts twisted but could see nothing. 'What?'

'Sarah Gilchrist just left with Mark Harrison, her ostrich farmer chap, without coming over to say hello.'

'Maybe she didn't see us,' Watts said.

'Maybe,' Grace said, certain Gilchrist had.

When they had ordered she leaned forward. 'Tell me about your friend in Lewes prison.'

'Pardon?' Watts said, surprised.

'Sarah and Bellamy told me when all that stuff was going on a couple of months ago that the breakthrough was your friend in Lewes prison identifying that man who came up to my house to attack me.'

'Graham Goody? Yes, he was my friend. He took a wrong turn.'

'How long is he serving?'

Watts shrugged. 'He's getting early release in a couple of years. In return for help he gave to us and other investigations, he has a much reduced sentence. Why do you ask?'

Grace shook her head. 'I was just curious how you would know a bank robber.'

'As I said: he took a wrong turn. He was in the SAS – with Jimmy Tingley actually. Good man in a scrape.'

'Could you trust him?'

'In a scrape? Absolutely.'

'Even today?'

'Yes – but Ms Grace, why are you asking?'

'We're not going to get very far if you're going to keep calling me Ms Grace.'

'Are we trying to get very far?'

Grace grinned that grin and sat back to let the waitress put her food in front of her. Sea bass for her; fillet steak for him. She raised her glass. *'Bon appetit.'*

Gilchrist drove back over to Brighton via Lewes and called Heap and Bilson en route. Neither were doing anything, so she suggested they meet for a late afternoon drink in the Cricketers. 'It's not a date,' she said to Bilson quickly.

She got caught up in traffic along the seafront, so both men were already in the pub when she finally arrived. A glass of Sauvignon Blanc awaited her.

'No, go on with what you were talking about,' she said, as they both turned to her when she sat down.

'I was remarking that everything is in *existential crisis* these days,' Bilson said. 'And I bet nobody who uses the term really knows what existentialism is or has ever heard of Kierkegaard, Camus or Sartre.'

'I bet Bellamy has,' Gilchrist said, looking over at him. It was unusual to see him casually dressed, in jeans and a polo shirt. Even more so Bilson, who was in corduroys and an open-neck chequered shirt.

'Well, that goes without saying,' Bilson said. 'Google is based on you, Bellamy, I would imagine.'

'More like Ask Jeeves,' Heap said. 'You know, a prototype.'

'Whatever happened to that?' Gilchrist said.

'Subsumed by something else,' Bilson said.

Heap said, 'The truth is always the truth, even if no one is using it. A lie is always a lie, even if everyone is using it.'

Bilson nodded. 'St Augustine – you were schooled by Jesuits, Bellamy?'

Heap shook his head. 'Nor am I a practising Catholic. Just interested in that stuff. You?'

'Nuns,' Bilson said. They both glanced at Gilchrist.

'Not me,' she said. 'Local comprehensive. Religious family, mind.'

'It didn't take?' Bilson said.

Gilchrist shook her head. 'Not my thing.'

'You don't believe in a Higher Power?' Bilson asked.

'You mean the chief constable?'

Bilson laughed. 'Along those lines, yes.'

Gilchrist shook her head. 'I don't really believe in her. Can't wait for her to go, actually.'

'I can understand that,' Bilson said. 'She doesn't seem to have much flair.'

'I think she's too conscious she's a woman in a senior job in a massively male culture,' Gilchrist said. 'She can't seem to relax into it, which is understandable. Except she has been doing it for some years now – since Bob Watts stepped down – you would have thought she'd have got the hang of it and relax a bit.'

'Where is Bob?' Bilson asked. 'Still in Canada?'

'I don't think he went in the end,' Gilchrist said. 'Actually, I've just seen him in the Jolly Sportsman in Plumpton with Nimue Grace.' She was still surprised by the sudden pang of jealousy she had felt when she saw them together.

'Jammy bugger,' Bilson said, shaking his head.

Gilchrist smiled. She was still thinking about Watts and Grace together. Were they having a thing? And why was she so bothered if they were?

'I've heard that Bob is being lined up for a new job,' Bilson said.

'What new job?' Gilchrist said, more sharply than she intended.

Bilson shook his head. 'No idea. But he is a bit wasted doing what he does.'

'A new job in Brighton?' Gilchrist said.

Bilson looked at her and paused before he answered. 'I don't know, Sarah. But I can't imagine he'd leave here – he's settled, isn't he?'

Gilchrist shrugged. Heap got up suddenly. 'My round.'

Bilson watched him then turned to Gilchrist. 'Is Bellamy OK? He seems rather abstracted.'

'He's got a bit obsessed with family history,' Gilchrist said. 'But he doesn't want to talk about it until it's concluded.'

'His family were coppers, weren't they? Chief constables and all that?'

'On his mother's side,' Gilchrist said. 'I think he's chasing up his dad's side.'

'That kind of thing interest you, Sarah?'

'I know more than I want to about my family to be perfectly honest,' Gilchrist said.

'I don't know anything about mine,' Bilson said. 'Children's homes all the way for me.'

'I'm sorry to hear that, Frank,' Gilchrist said. 'I had no idea.'

'Why would you? They didn't put a tattoo on my forehead or anything.'

'Even so.'

Heap came back and passed Bilson his drink.

'Now back to the matter in hand,' Bilson said. 'Have you tracked down the director, Cat Pinter, yet?'

'Disappeared.'

'Doesn't that concern you?'

'Of course it does,' Gilchrist said, sharp again. Bilson didn't seem to notice or chose to ignore it.

'Can I help in any way?' Bilson said mildly.

'Unless you've got a crystal ball or can communicate with her telepathically . . .'

'The likelihood is that she is dead. You know that.'

'I do know that is possible – but I hope not likely. I also know that our chief constable has told us to move on – we're not allowed to investigate further.'

Bilson cocked his head. 'I wouldn't have thought that would inhibit you, Sarah.'

Gilchrist looked out into the street, then at Bilson. 'Quite right, Frank. Quite right.' She looked at Heap. 'First thing tomorrow we go to the West End to see her agent.'

'What about our leads on the county lines thing?'

'Darren is still out cold and Kobel can wait a bit. We need to wrap this theatre murder up.'

Heap nodded slowly. 'All right, Sarah.' Gilchrist guessed he was calling her by her name because it was a Sunday and they were off-duty. 'But it's not the West End – she's in Hampstead Heath.'

'Really? I thought the West End was the hub of all this acting and theatre thing?'

'I assumed that too,' Heap said. 'But perhaps it's different for theatre directors' agents.'

THIRTEEN

Bellamy Heap was in charge of transport logistics. Next morning, they took the train up to Victoria then the Victoria line up to Highbury and Islington. He ushered Gilchrist onto the North London Line, an overground route that Gilchrist didn't even know existed. She felt guilty at her enjoyment peering into the back windows of all the houses they passed en route. They went west five stops and got out at Hampstead Heath. Except, Heap told Gilchrist, it was actually South End Green.

'Where's the Heath?' Gilchrist said as they came out onto a busy street.

Heap was looking off to his right. 'Just up there I think.'

'And the agency?'

Heap looked behind him. 'Up here. Parliament Hill.'

Parliament Hill was steep and Gilchrist showed undue interest in the architecture of the urban villas on either side of the road as she tried to hide the fact she was puffed. Slender Heap was, of course, like a mountain goat.

The house was almost at the top. They walked past it at first to the start of the Heath.

'That's Parliament Hill itself,' Heap said, pointing up a footpath between wooden fencing. 'The view is meant to be wonderful over London. Would you care to look?'

'So you can explain to me why it's called Parliament Hill? I don't think so.'

Heap giggled his curious, high-pitched giggle. 'Actually, I don't know why.'

Gilchrist stopped dramatically but, secretly, also because she was out of breath again. 'Bellamy! I rely on you as my source of all knowledge. What do you mean you don't know?'

Heap said nothing but pointed at the plaque on the wall of the villa they were standing in front of. 'George Orwell lived here for a couple of years.'

'I don't know and I don't want to know.'

'*Animal Farm*?'

'Oh, him.'

'*The Road to Wigan Pier*?'

'Stop while you're ahead, Bellamy. Is that the house over there?'

Gilchrist pointed and they walked diagonally across the road to a house with another plaque, this time to *Anna Wickham, feminist poet*. Gilchrist glanced at Heap. 'Don't smirk,' she said, 'just tell me.'

'A poem about marrying a man of the Croydon class and involving London clay, I believe, is much anthologized, but I know no more than that.'

'You're losing your power to impress today, Bellamy.'

'Ma'am,' Heap said as he pointed diagonally back down the road. 'We walked past the house we need.'

'Don't think you're going to salvage much with that,' Gilchrist said, as they went up a short front path to a large door with various doorbells.

'Here she is,' Heap said, pressing the bell of a flat with the name Olivia Oland on it.

'I was expecting a house,' Gilchrist said.

'I suspect the flats in these houses are quite big enough,' Heap said as a querulous voice came tinnily through the intercom.

'What?' the querulous voice said.

Gilchrist did the intros and explained why they were there.

'For God's sake,' the querulous voice said and the intercom went dead.

Gilchrist stretched out to press it again but Heap shook his head. A moment later there was a buzz and a click and Heap pressed against the large front door and they went in.

About ten yards down the wide corridor, a woman who might have stepped out of a late Bette Davis horror movie was standing in a doorway. Jowly, baggy-eyed, in a kind of dressing gown, her garishly red-lipsticked mouth clamped on a half-smoked cigarette, the smoke curling round her head.

She gestured with her head into her flat and turned back inside. Gilchrist noted she was wearing slippers. Gilchrist looked at Heap, who just smiled.

'Theatrical agenting isn't what it used to be when I was a director and trying to get representation,' Oland said, when they were seated on a collapsing sofa in her cluttered front room. 'There wasn't any.'

'But now there is?' Heap said.

'Me and about two others and we earn bugger all. Do you mind if I smoke?'

'You already are,' Gilchrist said.

Oland looked at her sharply. 'I *know* that, I was just being polite.'

'It's fine,' Gilchrist said. 'We wanted you to tell us about Cat Pinter.'

'I've told your colleagues I don't know where she is. And it's damned inconvenient. Not to mention costly. She was provisionally lined up for two more shows for quite good fees – and I would of course have got fifteen per cent of those.'

'Where might you guess she had gone?'

'I have no idea. I don't know anything about her personal life or her travels.'

'You don't know of any place in the UK that was a favourite of hers?'

Oland had finished her cigarette. She dropped it into the ashtray in front of her and reached for the cigarette packet beside it. As she lit up another one, Gilchrist looked around the room. Framed posters for theatre plays she'd never heard of on every wall between bookshelves. There were half a dozen unwashed wine glasses and a half-empty bottle of red wine with a stopper in the top on a tray on top of a bureau. Half empty or half full? Gilchrist always wavered on that.

Heap had seen the glasses. 'You've had a drinks reception? Is that a regular requirement for agents?'

Oland glanced over at the glasses. 'Last evening. I was just too lazy to clear up. Not a regular requirement, but I like to put people together.'

'Did Cat Pinter come to such things?'

'Occasionally.'

'Did she strike up any particular friendships?'

'Not that I'm aware of.'

'Do you know Elvira Wright?' Gilchrist said.

'I don't think anybody knew Elvira Wright. I understand she kept to herself. Very buttoned up. Why she acted, I suppose – she could express herself then. I only met her once.'

'At one of your parties?'

Oland nodded. 'Cat only ever brought others with her a couple of times. One was an actress called Felicity, who was far too sharp-eyed for my liking.'

'What do you mean?' Gilchrist said.

'Her eyes were never still – she was looking everywhere. I imagined her assessing everyone – or, more likely, looking for the main chance.'

'Do you remember her last name?'

Oland shook her head. 'I'm afraid not. So many eager actresses, so little time. She was probably buttering up Cat so Cat would use her in something.'

'And Cat brought Elvira too?'

'Not at the same time as that Felicity person. It was a few weeks later. Just before they went into rehearsals for *The Dinner Game*. That's the first and last time I met her.'

'Anything happen at that time that might be useful to us?'

Oland took a long drag on her cigarette and squinted as she blew out a plume of smoke. 'I don't want to be gossipy, but I thought they might be having a thing.' She waved the cigarette vaguely. 'I mean, I don't know the sexuality of either of them and these days it's complicated but I just got the impression . . .'

There was a sudden thump on the ceiling as if something had been dropped. Oland looked up in annoyance. 'New tenant just moved in,' she said, taking another long drag on her cigarette.

'You rent here?' Gilchrist asked.

'No, no. I own the house and I rent out the two floors above.'

There was another thump.

'It's been in the family since the 1920s. There used to be cattle grazing on the Heath back then for the London meat markets. My grandfather bought it when he married. Nothing to do with cattle. He was a surveyor but also a minor poet.' She waved at a bookcase. 'I've got his collections there some-where, alongside those of my grandmother – she was quite a successful poet in the thirties too. I tried to get a blue plaque for them like the ones up the street but it was rejected – cutbacks and all that stuff. Never a good idea, two poets living together. Look at Ted and Sylvia.'

'Indeed,' Heap said. 'My partner is doing a writing workshop in their home in Heptonstall at the moment.'

'Lumb Bank? Nice there but the weather can be fierce. Ted was the more successful of that couple but with my grandparents it was my grandmother. Feminist critics have long made a case for him trying to discourage her or undermine her.' She gestured vaguely up the street. 'She drowned herself in the Ladies' Pond up on the Heath. You a poet then?'

'Not in the proper sense. How did your grandfather cope?' Heap asked.

'Not well. Depending on my mood, I'm never sure if he too committed suicide or died in an accident down your way – at the Seven Sisters.'

'When was this?' Heap said. Gilchrist looked at him – she recognized that tone in his voice. Heap used it when he was on the scent of something.

'1938,' Oland said. 'Edith drowned herself the year before.'

All very interesting, Gilchrist thought, but irrelevant. 'How many clients have you got?' she said, to get back on track.

'Only six these days. I'm winding down.' Oland gestured vaguely around her. 'And, to be honest, I don't need to work at all with the rental I get from the flats upstairs.'

'And this house in this wonderful location must be worth a bob or two,' Gilchrist said.

'But I'd never sell it,' Oland said, sounding a little shocked.

'Do you have family to leave it to?' Gilchrist asked.

Oland looked at her sharply. 'Is that any of your business?'

Gilchrist was embarrassed. 'I'm sorry – force of habit asking intrusive questions.'

'I never had the motherhood gene, if that's what you were asking, Detective Inspector,' Oland said, seemingly mollified. 'Do you have it?'

'I don't think so,' Gilchrist said, squirming a little.

Heap came to her rescue. 'Can you give us the details of your other clients, especially if they were at that drinks party which Elvira attended.'

'Well, I don't remember who exactly was at that particular party,' Oland said. 'But I can give you my clients' details. Do you want them now?'

'If possible,' Heap said.

Oland went over to the bureau, her slippers flapping. Her dressing gown at the back had caught in the cleft of her buttocks. She rooted in the top drawer. She came up with a single sheet of paper.

'Their details are here.'

'We'll be in touch if we need any more information,' Gilchrist said, as she and Heap stood.

Heap handed Oland his card. She looked at it blankly. 'In case you hear from Cat Pinter.'

'Of course,' she finally said.

Out in the street Gilchrist looked at Heap. 'What interested you about Oland's grandfather's death?'

'Oh, just curiosity,' Heap said. 'As I said, I'm a bit obsessed with family histories at the moment. Shall we walk over to Belsize Park Tube to get back to a railway station to take us back to Sussex?'

As they started down the steep street, Gilchrist said: 'Do you think Cat Pinter and Elvira Wright were an item?'

'Perhaps we can check with the other actors in *The Dinner Game*,' Heap said. 'Though I suspect it's the backstage people who will know more – I'm told they don't miss a thing.'

'I'll get DC Wade to check with *Spotlight* and Equity again whether there's a way to trace this Felicity with just her first name.'

A few moments later as they came to the bottom of the steep road, he gestured across the road. 'Isn't that Bob Watts going into the pub?'

'Talking of not missing a thing.' Gilchrist watched as Bob Watts, arm in arm with a lithe young woman, went into the pub.

'Should we go and say hello?' Heap said. Gilchrist gave him a look. He flushed. 'No, you're right. We'd better crack on.'

But then Watts came out of the pub with the young woman and saw them standing across the street.

'Oh, hello,' Gilchrist called and she and Heap walked towards them. 'This is a surprise. I gather you didn't go to Canada.'

'Our plans changed after Morocco,' Watts said, looking uncomfortable. Gilchrist was looking at the tall, attractive young woman beside Watts. 'Oh, this is Margaret. Margaret Lively. Margaret, this is my friend and former colleague, DI Sarah Gilchrist.'

The two women shook hands perfunctorily, giving each other the once-over.

'And DS Bellamy Heap,' Watts said. Heap and Lively nodded to each other.

'What brings you here?' Watts said.

'Routine enquiries. You?'

'We were hoping to get some lunch in the Magdala here but the chef is ill so no food today. This is the pub where Ruth Ellis shot her lover – the last woman hanged in Britain?' Watts gestured back at the pub. 'You're supposed to be able to see a bullet hole from her shooting spree in this outside wall somewhere.'

'You didn't tell me that,' Lively said.

'I was saving it for meal-time useless information.'

'I meant what were you doing in the neighbourhood,' Gilchrist said.

'Oh we went for a swim in the mixed pond up on the Heath.' Watts gave a pretend shiver. 'Bracing is the word I'd use.'

Heap glanced over at the North London line track in the gully on the other side of the road. 'That's our train coming, ma'am. We should make a move.'

They made their excuses and goodbyes and hurried down the street to the station. 'We're not going via Belsize Park then?'

'I thought perhaps a quick getaway might be better,' Heap said, as they hurried down the steps onto the platform.

'Wise man,' Gilchrist murmured as they reached the platform just before the doors of the train started to close.

They reversed their route back to Victoria and caught a Brighton train within minutes. Once again the train journey didn't lull Gilchrist to sleep. Instead, she gazed out of the window and tried to think through where they were at with this investigation. Maybe a few inches further forward. She knew that when she got back to Brighton she needed to focus on county lines drugs. But first, she thought, a visit to the Theatre Royal scene of the crime might be in order.

However, what really kept distracting her was the sight of Bob Watts with the young woman just a day after she'd seen him with Nimue Grace. What was going on with him? More to the point, why was she feeling so jealous?

FOURTEEN

B ob Watts and Margaret Lively had settled in the Railway Tavern, an old Victorian pub on South End Green just the other side of the railway track. It had a large courtyard garden and they were under an outdoor heater in the far corner.

'You don't want my help to get William Simpson anymore?' Lively said, picking up a forkful of her Cobb salad.

'You've already helped me to see the way forward,' Watts said, putting his own fork down. 'There is no need to involve yourself further.'

Lively looked at him, her fork full of lettuce poised in mid-air. She put the food in her mouth, still watching him.

'Just between us, because it's not public yet,' Watts said, 'I've been offered a job with the National Crime Agency.' Lively chewed her food, eyes never leaving his face. 'And it has a file open on William Simpson. They're onto him.' Watts shrugged. 'So I can be doing this through official – OK, semi-official – channels. No need for you to be embroiled in it.'

'You think the NCA have any clue what they're doing?' Lively said quietly, dabbing her lips with her napkin. 'The government has appointed as head of its Intelligence Committee a man who, when last in government, gave a lucrative ferry contract to a company with no ferries and no experience. He also privatized the probation service with disastrous results. Let's not even start on the railways.' She shook her head. 'Anyway, I am embroiled in it, Bob.'

'What do you mean?' Watts said. 'You told me—'

'That I'm not involved with Simpson's money laundering? Perfectly true. But somebody doesn't believe that. And from what you've just told me it's the NCA that is bugging me.'

'Bugging you?'

'Surely they told you that as part of your job interview?' Watts grimaced and nodded.

'When were you going to tell me?' She gave a small smile.

'Were you going to tell me?' She laughed at his perplexed expression. 'Bob, one of the things I like about you is that for such a high-stepper you are *so* lacking in guile.'

'Probably today,' Watts almost stuttered. 'I was probably going to tell you today. I was trying to work out how best to break it to you. But you already knew?'

'I used to be a bit of a techie when I was a student and several of my friends from university have made it their life. And one of them is a bit of a rebel. Believes in openness and all that. He's paranoid too, of course. That goes with the territory in this age of the Deep State. Paranoid on my behalf too.'

'He discovered you were bugged?'

'Months ago. Knowing that, I've not touched the bugs but have acted accordingly.' She smiled mischievously. 'Except in the bedroom.'

'What about in the bedroom? They bugged your bedroom?'

'I know – do they have no dignity, these people you're going to work for? I assume they thought I might be making the beast with two backs with Simpson. Which means their Intel can't be that good, since I thought it was obvious he was into young men.'

'What did you do with that bug?' Watts asked, trying to be nonchalant.

'I don't know what the technical term is but, rest assured, what they are hearing is not what goes on in my bedroom – so I'm afraid your prowess is not preserved for posterity. Well, except for that sex tape I shot of us.' She saw his look and took another forkful of food. 'I'm joking, Bob, you adorable man.'

'I knew that,' he said, unconvincingly, so out of his depth he didn't know which way to turn.

'Sure you did.' She looked arch. 'So, not using me to help nail William Simpson – does that mean you don't mean to use me at all?'

Even Watts understood that. 'Definitely not,' he said firmly. 'I mean I definitely do want to . . . you know.'

'Then best eat up, Police Commissioner, because I feel another marathon coming on.'

*   *   *

Nimue Grace was in her usual workshirt and jeans figuring out where to thin out her thick bed of lavender so the lavender wouldn't choke itself. Bees and butterflies flew around her before settling again on the plant. She laughed to herself at the thought she was in an old Walt Disney cartoon.

But, then again, it was a magical garden. Only a few minutes earlier she had watched a young fox wandering through the orchard. It had seen her, assessed her and carried on, fearless. Insects were whizzing by – she loved the zip and zap of them.

Graham Goody wouldn't be released anytime soon, that much she had got from Bob Watts. Bob Watts – he was an odd one. She was willing herself to find him attractive when he wasn't her usual type. The different parts of him – intelligence, probity, bravery – were all interesting and, indeed, admirable, but the sum of his parts just didn't add up for her.

She sighed. No point worrying about a future mate now. She had never felt the need for one to be honest. She was very happy on her own. She wouldn't go as far as – what was that silly word someone in Brighton had come up with, though she'd heard it from a silly young actress? Sologamy. A silly word for a silly concept.

The actress – Grace couldn't even remember her name – had been moaning about her love life. 'I really want to be married with kids, old-fashioned as that sounds.'

'You just haven't met the right man,' Grace said, hoping she was hiding her boredom.

'Well, I had a man and he was no good and he broke my heart. And I met a man who was really, really good and I broke his heart. What about you, Nimue – have you ever considered marrying yourself?'

'No, never,' Grace said.

'No, I mean, have you tried marrying *yourself*?'

'I don't understand.'

'Sologamy.' Grace stifled a quip. 'It's the act of marrying yourself. It started in Brighton – no surprise there perhaps. Travelling alone; taking yourself out on dates. But you can actually marry yourself – it's a civil ceremony, obviously. It's a tongue-in-cheek statement about the stigma of being single.'

'Is there a stigma?' Grace said. 'I hadn't noticed. Surely there is more of a stigma about being childless?'

'Well, there is a link, of course. A perceived link. But with sologamy, you prioritize your relationship with yourself. It's a celebration of your own happiness in adult life. Wouldn't work for me but it might be right for you.'

'Thank you,' Grace had said politely. 'I'll bear it in mind.'

Gilchrist pulled open the stage door to the Theatre Royal and she and Heap walked into the gloom. There was an old wooden booth to the right, where a young woman sat at a computer. She stood and slid open one section of its glass front. Gilchrist told her their business and she gestured to them to go down the steep concrete corridor while she phoned the stage manager to say they were on their way.

The stage manager, Philippa Drake, met them at the side of the stage beside some kind of control desk. She was a short woman in her fifties dressed, all in black, but with bright orange hair and orange spectacles. After introductions she saw Gilchrist glancing at the control desk.

'That's where everything happens on the evening of a show.' She indicated the walkie-talkie and the headphones. 'They link to the sound and light mixing board at the back of the auditorium, and to front-of-house and the dressing rooms, so we can coordinate curtain up.

'Actors in the dressing rooms get various timed warnings so they don't miss their cues. Then they stand at one or other side of the stage before they come on – though some like to watch their fellow performers from the side anyway.'

'And do the actors usually obey?' Heap asked.

'If they're pros, they do. They know to get onstage when we tell them to. If they try to act like the Big I Am, it doesn't go down well.'

'What about a star like Billie Grahame?'

'A pro and very attentive to the tech crew – especially lighting.' She saw Gilchrist's puzzled look. 'Good lighting is essential for an actress of a certain age – a lighting technician can make someone look wonderful or hideous. That's often when the prima donnas who are rude to the technicians come a cropper – never underestimate the power of the lighting engineer once you're onstage.'

'And Elvira Wright?'

'Watching her fellow performers? No, no. She was too *in character* for that. Spent most of her time backstage shuffling up and down with her Zimmer frame.'

'And she took her position before that second act curtain on time and in the correct place?'

'She usually stood there for the whole interval. And, yes, always in the exact spot, front centre stage.'

'May we look?' Gilchrist said.

'Of course,' Drake said, leading them onstage. The curtains were up, so both Gilchrist and Heap had a full view of the auditorium and the ornate balconies. Gilchrist was surprised by how close to the stage the boxes at each side were.

She looked up at the gantry running across the stage. Drake followed her look. 'That's where it fell from,' Drake said. 'But I've no idea why it was there.'

'What?' Gilchrist said. 'I thought it was part of the pulley system for raising the fire curtain?'

Drake gestured to both sides of the stage – stage left and stage right, Heap had advised Gilchrist they were called. 'The weights come down at each side of the stage to raise the fire curtain up.'

'Of course,' Gilchrist murmured. It wouldn't be very handy to have an iron weight dangling centre stage while a play is being performed. She felt a flush of embarrassment that she hadn't thought of that. She glanced at Heap – neither had he. Heap didn't look back but blushed. 'So how did it get up there?'

'Somebody put it there, obviously. And you can't really see that gantry during showtime, as it's so high up. Or anybody up there, if they were wearing black – which we all do backstage.'

'How do you get up there?' Heap said.

Drake gestured again to both sides of the stage. 'Those ladders clamped to the walls.'

'Can we go up and have a look?'

'Your forensic people have already given it a thorough examination,' Drake said.

'Even so,' Gilchrist said. 'How's your vertigo, DS Heap?'

'Under control, ma'am. Why don't I go up stage right and

you go up stage left and we'll meet in the middle. Would you care to join us, Ms Drake.'

'Sure, though I don't know why.'

Gilchrist didn't have vertigo, but the climb up the iron ladder was hard work. She paused at the top when she stepped onto the gantry to catch her breath. She looked down. OK, maybe she did have vertigo. Goodness, the stage was a long way below.

The gantry shifted a little when she started to walk across it to meet the other two, who had already reached the middle. Drake saw the look on her face and smiled. 'It's OK,' she called. 'It always does that, but it's perfectly safe.'

'I'll believe you,' Gilchrist said when she reached them. She looked down again, gripping the guardrail tightly.

'Did you see the inscription on the brick wall as you came up the ladder?' Drake said brightly.

'My attention was on not falling,' Gilchrist said with a nervous laugh.

'It's not really an inscription – just initials, actually, carved out with a knife, with the date 1854. Although the theatre dates back to 1807. I'm guessing 1854 is the date the ladders and this iron gantry were put in when Charles Phipps expanded and redeveloped the old theatre.'

'Charles Phipps?' Gilchrist said, looking up at the roof beams instead of down at the stage. It didn't help.

'The theatre architect who made the theatre look as it does today.'

'I thought that was Frank Somebody?' Gilchrist said, remembering what Bilson had said.

'Frank Matcham? No, not this one, though he did lots of other wonderful theatres – the one in Richmond, Surrey is probably my favourite.'

Bilson wrong about the theatre architects; Bellamy not thinking through the lead weight – what were the know-it-alls Gilchrist relied on coming to?

Drake pointed down to the lower rail of the gantry. 'I assume it was tied to this somehow.'

'The weight?' Gilchrist said, glancing at Heap.

'Well, yes. Then all the killer had to do was untie it and get back down in the backstage kerfuffle as Elvira was hit with it.'

Gilchrist frowned, wondering why Bilson or SOCO hadn't come up with this hypothesis. She already knew the answer Bilson would give – that was her job, not his. She was kicking herself for not investigating backstage before.

'Did nobody interview you after this happened?'

'I wasn't here – I was on holiday until yesterday.'

'Anywhere nice?' Heap asked, surprising Gilchrist.

'Avignon – do you know it?'

Heap shook his head. 'When did you go?'

'Oh, a couple of days before this happened. It was just a short break. I didn't hear about it until I got back. It was quite a shock, I can tell you.'

'I can imagine. Your assistant' – Heap glanced at Gilchrist – 'DC Wade interviewed her, ma'am – didn't say anything about this.'

'I'm not high enough in the hierarchy to have an assistant. My stand-in, you mean. Flick Steadman. She does props. I imagine she was in shock, as I would have been.' Drake paused for a moment. 'And that the police would know the correct questions to ask.'

Bullseye. Gilchrist cleared her throat. 'So you think the weight would have needed to be tied to this and then released.'

'I'm just going off crime stuff I've read and seen on telly. It would need to be lined up properly, so I would have thought that needed to be in advance – couldn't risk getting it wrong on the night and all that.'

'But where did it come from in the first place?' Gilchrist said, still gripping tightly to the rail that, she noticed, Heap was leaning nonchalantly against. The bastard. But then he was shorter, she thought meanly, so there wasn't so much of him above the rail.

'Oh, we have half a dozen hanging from the walls. Sometimes they're needed for other heavy curtains with scenery painted on in more lavish productions than this one, or as spares for the fire curtain ones. Though usually these days, it's electric pulleys.'

'This production wasn't very lavish, was it?' Gilchrist murmured, risking a glance down at the stage far below, then pulling back.

'You can say that again,' Drake said. 'It didn't start like that. We had sofas, a dinner table, chairs, chandeliers and candelabras – and food – the play is all set around meals after all.'

'I didn't see enough of it to notice,' Gilchrist said, wondering what kind of mess she would make down on the stage if she threw up now. 'Perhaps we could continue this conversation back on the ground?'

Gilchrist found herself trembling as she started to climb back down the iron ladder. Her feet scrabbled nervously to get a good purchase on the next rung below and she clung on to every rung above with clenched hands as if her life depended on it – which she felt it did.

When she landed back on earth she thrust her hands in her pockets so Heap and Drake couldn't see them shaking. 'Shall we sit down somewhere?' she said, more loudly than she intended.

Drake looked at her oddly then led her to a door onto a short flight of stairs that went up to a long corridor. She opened a door on the right and gestured to them to enter what turned out to be one of the boxes overlooking the stage just some twenty feet away. There were four chairs and Gilchrist sat down gratefully in the one nearest the stage.

She gestured to Drake to sit beside her. Heap sat in the chair on the other side of the stage manager. He said: 'You were saying about the dinner table and chandeliers . . .'

'Well, the set designer, the props master and the stage manager work closely together when it comes to mounting a show and Flick, the props master for this show – she was my holiday stand-in, as I said – was telling me that no sooner had she sourced something or had it made than the director, Cat Pinter, discarded it. OK, she was complaining really. You should talk to Billie Grahame – she's very funny about it.'

Heap nodded. 'Going back to the gantry, Ms Drake – so you think it quite possible that someone could be up there unnoticed.'

'Certainly.'

'But can the same be said for going up and coming back down?'

'If they went up an hour before the show, definitely they

could. There would be hardly anyone about and stage right would be deserted.'

'And coming down?'

'I would imagine that would be more difficult.' She grinned. 'But aren't I doing your job for you?'

'You did say you like reading crime novels,' Gilchrist said. 'We thought you might like to have a think about it.'

'Well, then . . . perhaps nobody noticed the person coming down in all the chaos that ensued. Perhaps the person actually joined the others in fussing over the victim.'

'That would have to be somebody who works backstage, to get away with not standing out,' Gilchrist said.

'Well, in a *Poirot* set in the theatre, it would be somebody in the production,' Drake said.

Gilchrist smiled. 'You're right.' She stood. 'OK, thank you, Ms Drake. We'll be in touch if we need you anymore.' She gestured to Heap, who handed over his card. 'And if you think of anything, please do get in touch with us.'

Drake nodded and stood.

'Do you think we can go out through the front of the theatre?' Gilchrist said.

'Of course,' Drake said. 'When we come out of the box, just follow this corridor round the other way and take the stairs down into the back of the foyer.'

As they walked down the stairs, Gilchrist looked at her watch. 'Let's regroup in the Colonnade over a drink and a bite to eat. What do you think, Bellamy?'

'As long as crisps and peanuts are on offer.'

'Bellamy, I always took you to be a healthy eater!'

'They were for you, ma'am.'

'Ha! Well, you can fuck off, Bellamy,' Gilchrist said, as they went in to the ornate Victorian bar right beside the theatre.

Over her Sauvignon Blanc and his half of bitter from Harvey's, the Lewes brewery, they tried to figure out where they were. With crisps and peanuts, of course.

'What did you make of what Drake had to say?' Gilchrist said.

'I thought she said some very pertinent things,' Heap said, sipping his beer.

'You seemed very interested in her holiday, Bellamy.'

'Yes, ma'am. I thought it was convenient. And I also wondered who she might have been on holiday with.'

'For instance?'

'Oh, for instance, Cat Pinter.'

Gilchrist tilted her head and looked at Heap. 'Have you got some theory and you're doing a Poirot on me?'

'No, ma'am. Just inchoate thoughts swirling around.'

'*Inchoate*? Don't bloody *inchoate* me, Bellamy.'

'Sorry, ma'am. Maybe I should have simply said I have no ideas of any use.'

'Simply always works best with me.'

'Yes, ma'am.'

Gilchrist thought for a moment. 'All that stuff about not using props – do you think Pinter could have been embezzling money from that budget and that's why she's run away – if she has run away.'

'I don't quite get you,' Heap said.

'Well, there would be a budget for props and sets presumably. Reducing both to nothing would mean that money wasn't spent – but where is it?'

Heap frowned. 'I'm not sure how that would work, ma'am. I assume each section head would be responsible for their own budget.'

'Well, we're back to Drake going on her hols at a convenient moment. With Pinter and the money she embezzled.'

'It's feasible, I suppose,' Heap said slowly. 'Although Drake said that Flick said that Pinter was discarding stuff already bought.'

Gilchrist looked glum. 'You mean I'm clutching at straws.'

'Not at all, ma'am. We need to keep everything on the table. But I'm not sure how that line of reasoning gets us nearer to Elvira's murderer.'

Gilchrist sipped her wine then picked up her phone. 'I want to know why Bilson didn't see the obvious.'

'None of us saw the obvious, ma'am. The main thing, though, is what we do now with the little new knowledge we have.'

Gilchrist nodded. 'Maybe we should get Sylvia Wade here. Maybe there was something in her interviews we didn't pick up on.'

'We have the transcripts, ma'am.'

'Yes, but we need to know what Sylvia saw on people's faces.'

'Indeed, ma'am.'

Gilchrist looked glum again. 'How did I drop the ball on this?'

'I think you've been very energetic, ma'am. It's more of a conundrum than we normally have to deal with. All that stuff surrounding Nimue Grace a couple of months ago just required old-fashioned dogged police work – questioning people and finding links and straightforward tedious work.'

'And a bit of inspiration from you.'

Heap waved that away. 'Not inspired enough to figure out where the rest of the Hassocks Blockade money went.'

'No offence, Bellamy, but I don't think that's a priority just now either.' Gilchrist reached for her phone. 'Mr Bilson,' she said, 'that was a quick pick-up.'

'Why are you surprised? You know I sit around each day just waiting for your call.'

'Ha – even you can't expect me to fall for that one. The stage manager at the theatre has just pointed out the obvious.'

'Always refreshing.'

'The weight can't have been attached to the fire curtain in the middle of it.'

Bilson was quiet for a moment then laughed. 'Yes. I see. Obvious indeed. So it was tied to the gantry and then released from there. Of course, that doesn't really take you any further forward.'

'Have you any other thoughts?'

'When you bring me something to think about I will. I can't make bread without whatever it is you can't make bread without.'

'Isn't that making bricks without something or other?' Gilchrist said.

'Not a sandwich without butter?'

'You can have lots of sandwiches without butter. Tuna, for instance. Peanut butter.'

'Well, that goes without saying,' Bilson said. 'The peanut butter. The clue is in the name of the spread. Mind you, there's a whole debate about Marmite.'

'So I understand,' Gilchrist said.

'No, not that one. I mean as in whether you use butter before you spread the Marmite or no butter.'

'OK, well, I think you can make bread without pretty much anything these days and still call it bread. Especially in Brighton. So, thanks, Frank.'

When she put the phone down, she said: 'I wonder if Nimue Grace would help us meet Billie Grahame in a more informal setting.'

'You think she has more to offer?'

'I think you said she was a bit vague about when she'd last seen Cat Pinter.'

'Sure, ma'am,' Heap said. 'But perhaps we should move along with the county lines drug inquiry first.'

Gilchrist sighed. 'I know, I know. OK. We should call on Liesl Rabbitt at the big house in Plumpton. Try to talk to Kobel. Call the community policeman there – PC Edwards, is it these days? – and ask him to pick us up.'

'That's quite an ancient Sussex name: Rabbitt,' Heap said. 'It came over with the Normans when they invaded and introduced rabbits to this country. Or I thought they introduced them.'

'Really?' Gilchrist said, only half listening as she thought about Bob Watts and Nimue Grace and Margaret Lively.

'I was at Fishbourne recently – do you know it?'

'The Roman palace down near Chichester?' Gilchrist said, dragging herself away from her thoughts. 'I've heard of it.'

'They've just radiocarbon dated a bone unearthed there. A rabbit's tibia bone. It dates back to 1AD. That's 1,065 years before the Normans invaded. It was found in 1964 but nobody identified it then and it was left in a box. Then in 2017, a zooarchaeologist recognized it for what it was.'

'Really?' Gilchrist repeated, her mind now going back to this theatre death, which she just didn't want to let go. 'Zooarchaeologist, eh?'

'They think it was a pet in the palace's menagerie.'

'Really?' Gilchrist said again.

When Heap phoned and told Edwards where he needed to take them he said: 'I was just about to go there, sir.'

'Has something happened?' Gilchrist said.

'There's a body in an ice block – I think it's fallen out of the sky in Mrs Rabbitt's garden. A stowaway on a flight to Gatwick, I assume, ma'am.'

'Fell out of the plane when the wheels went down?' Gilchrist said.

'That's right, ma'am. It's not the first case around Gatwick, though it is the first in this specific area.'

Gilchrist turned to Heap when she had ended the call. 'See, I told you the sky is not to be trusted.'

'You were referring then to rather unusual circumstances,' Heap said. 'You don't generally expect fish to fall out of the sky or indeed to be clobbered by a hail of dead birds.'

The reference was to a strange summer when Heap first became a team with Gilchrist. They were investigating apparently Satanic goings-on around Brighton. At the time of the investigation, a tornado out at sea had scooped up fish and deposited them in a heavy hail over Brighton. Gilchrist herself had been injured by a large cod, which is not a story she shared anymore because of the laughter it always inspired.

Many people thought the hail of fish was a sign, from God or the Devil – these people were pretty much evenly split as to which. But as Bilson had drummed into them on many occasions, this had been coincidence not causality. Freakish nevertheless.

'Should we check with Mr Blackstone of the NCA about Kobel?' Heap said. 'See if he knows anything?'

Gilchrist nodded, speed-dialled Blackstone and put the call on speaker so Heap could listen. 'We're on our way to try to talk to an Albanian called Kobel, who might be the kingpin of the Sussex county lines drug thing. We wondered if you had any Intel—'

'I'd rather you didn't,' Blackstone said.

'You'd rather we didn't talk to him?' Gilchrist said. 'Because?'

'His story is bigger than just Sussex. We've had a watching brief on him for a while hoping to identify all the links in the chain that take it back to the source – or sources, of course.'

'But you asked us to find out who the puppet masters are.'

'And I believe you've found Darren's handler. We're aware of Clive Pyne. Work sideways from him. Look, we're right in the middle of something that might have put the frighteners on Kobel. We've just arrested six hundred people in coordinated raids across the rest of the country.

'We got drugs, teenage gang members and weapons. And we rescued over five hundred people whose homes had been cuckooed by dealers.'

'Why weren't we involved?' Gilchrist said.

'Because we're doing you next, Detective Inspector. The National County Lines Coordination Centre organized it. You'll hear from them soon, rest assured. But it was a reminder to be careful dealing with these people. Nationally we seized guns, swords, machetes, axes, knives and a couple of crossbows.'

Gilchrist ended the call. Heap shrugged. 'They want to keep us in a little box down here,' he said.

Gilchrist nodded. 'Let's still go and see Mrs Liesl Rabbitt anyway.'

Edwards drove confidently through the twisting, narrow Sussex lanes and up the long drive to Rabbitt's house. Gilchrist glanced over as they passed Beard's Pond, Nimue Grace's lake, on their left. Further up the drive, she saw that Mark Harrison was correct. There was no sign of llamas in the fields closer to the Georgian pile they were approaching.

Liesl Rabbitt, hard-faced and brusque as ever, met them at the entrance to the grand Georgian house. She grimaced.

'You two? I'm not surprised you've been demoted. So now you're reduced to investigating frozen men?'

Gilchrist clenched her jaw. 'We came to ask about Mr Kobel. He lives here?'

'No,' Rabbitt said shortly.

'You know him?'

'A little bit. Why?'

'He stays here sometimes?' Gilchrist said.

'Why you want to know? My private life is my private life.'

'Is he here now?'

Rabbitt shook her head. 'In Albania. Family emergency.' She gestured over to a stretch of lawn. 'What you going to do about

Ice Man? I was sunbathing. He might have landed on me. I'm traumatized. Who do I sue?'

Gilchrist and Heap walked over and looked down at the ice-block body. African probably. 'Well, not him,' Gilchrist said. She took Heap's arm and led him away a few yards. 'Keep her busy while I go into the house for a minute.'

'We have no search warrant, ma'am,' Heap warned.

'I'm just going to find a toilet, that's all. And who knows who I might bump into?'

Liesl Rabbitt watched as Gilchrist headed back toward the community police car parked in front of the entrance to the house. 'Just getting something from the car, Mrs Rabbitt,' Gilchrist called. 'DS Heap wants to have a word with you about this and potential compensation.'

Rabbitt started towards Heap as Gilchrist hurried past the car, putting her finger to her lips as PC Edwards looked questioningly at her. She went up the half a dozen steps and into the house through the half-open door.

'This is more rare than unusual, Mrs Rabbitt,' Heap said, as she came up to him. 'I think we can assume this poor person stowed away in the undercarriage of a plane, froze to death on the journey – which suggests it was medium to long-haul – and then fell out when the plane's landing gear opened as it approached Gatwick. It's not the first time this kind of thing has happened with people desperate to get to the West.'

'Gatwick?' Mrs Rabbitt said. 'So I sue Gatwick?'

'Mrs Rabbitt, I don't imagine you can sue anybody,' Heap said. 'It's nothing to do with Gatwick. But, let me reiterate, I don't believe you'll be able to sue anybody.'

Rabbitt snorted. 'That's all you know. You can always sue somebody. Especially in this debased country.'

'Well, then, I suppose it's either going to be the airline or the airport of origin,' Heap said. 'People are on their way to clear this up, Mrs Rabbit.' Heap looked up at the house and immediately looked away when he saw Gilchrist coming back down the steps. 'So you're staying on here?'

'For the sake of the children,' Rabbitt simpered. 'What else can I do?'

'And Tallulah Granger, the late Mr Rabbitt's sister?'

'Well, since we wound up the Airbnb here – I could never understand why my husband would want strangers wandering around his home – she has no reason to be here. She's moved back to her poky house in Oxford and will presumably get a proper job.'

'And your proper job?' Heap said. 'The café in Lewes?'

Mrs Rabbitt smiled coldly. 'My *proper* job is to be a mother and *chatelaine* of this great house. My friend – you met her – has taken over the café – I rent it to her.'

'Very organized,' Gilchrist said as she rejoined them. 'Does your friend know Mr Kobel?'

'We Albanians stick together, so of course,' Rabbitt said.

'I thought you were part Greek,' Gilchrist said.

'We Greeks stick together too,' Rabbitt said with a sniff. She looked Gilchrist up and down. 'You've put on weight – is that from hanging out with that cray-cray ostrich farmer and eating too many omelettes?'

'We'll be in touch when we have more information, Mrs Rabbitt,' Gilchrist said, turning away.

'People are on their way,' Heap said again. 'Goodbye, Mrs Rabbitt.'

Rabbitt smirked. 'Just let me know which airline to sue for my mental distress.'

'God, I loathe that woman,' Gilchrist said as Edwards drove them down the drive.

'Anything in the house, ma'am?'

Gilchrist shook her head. 'Nobody about.' As they drove past Grace's lake again she said to Edwards: 'Stop a minute.' Gilchrist got out of the car and walked over to the Victorian fencing at this end of the lake. 'Bellamy, there are turtles here – come and look!'

Heap exited the car and came to stand beside Gilchrist. She pointed at two turtles the size of dinner plates sitting on a large, flat rock, their brightly coloured necks extended and their heads moving from side to side.

'Overgrown terrapins,' Heap said. 'Some parents would have dumped them in here when their kid got fed up playing Ninja Turtles. Ms Grace should be told, in case she doesn't already know. They eat little ducklings, which will play havoc with her breeding programme here.' He looked across towards the lily pads. 'And there's an angry-looking swan over there giving us the eye.'

They got back in the car. 'That's Ms Grace's lake, isn't it?' Edwards said.

'It is,' Gilchrist said, as Heap checked his phone.

'There's been a report of sheep rustling in the field next door to her property. We're used to lampers around here' – Edwards saw her look – 'poaching by lamplight. But this is slaughtering and butchering on site, leaving the carcases and taking the meat away.'

'Sheep rustling.'

'Yes, ma'am, but at a different level. I was going to question her, but since you're here—'

Heap interrupted. 'So a plane spotter has footage of the body falling when the wheels were lowered. A Kenya Airlines plane on a nine-hour, 4,250-mile flight, with temperatures for this poor man dropping to as low as minus sixty.'

'That's desperation for you,' Gilchrist said. 'What would make him take such a massive risk?'

'We may never know, ma'am. There's no guarantee he will ever be identified. Where now?'

Gilchrist nodded to Edwards. 'Let's call in on Nimue Grace to warn her about the terrapins and the crazy swan, and ask her about the bloody sheep. And let's see if she can give us a hand with Billie Grahame.'

FIFTEEN

Gilchrist and Heap got no answer when they rang the bell at Nimue Grace's. Their phone call went unanswered too. While Gilchrist went back to the car to check in with HQ, Heap went to the side door to Grace's garden. It was unlocked, so he tentatively pushed it open.

He saw Grace in a lounger, some kind of pamphlet in her hand. 'Ms Grace?' he called tentatively.

She looked up and put the pamphlet down. 'What are you doing here?'

'We phoned and got no reply and rang the bell on the front door and the same thing. Sorry to intrude.'

She sat up and beckoned for him to come in. 'The bell doesn't work. Battery gone or something. Well, it's very nice to see you. But why am I seeing you?'

'It's about some stolen sheep. DI Gilchrist will explain when she comes in – she's just on the phone.'

'Stolen sheep?' She looked under her chair. 'Nope, not me – not guilty. You know, the first smugglers were here hundreds of years ago, on the flats over where Derek Jarman's house is. They were known as owlers, though nobody really knows why.' She swung up out of her chair and stood, significantly taller than Bellamy Heap. 'Do you want a cuppa? I was just going to put the kettle on.'

Heap shook his head. 'But you carry on,' he said, walking alongside her back to the house. 'You like history, Ms Grace?'

'It fascinates me.' She gestured back to her chair. 'I was just reading about the Spanish armadas in Sussex in a pamphlet from the local historian who lives down the other end of the drive. Did you know there were actually three armadas sent to invade England? After the famous one, they tried again in 1596 and again in 1597 but the same thing happened as with the one in 1588.'

'Walter Raleigh?'

'No – terrible storms in the Bay of Biscay. Shipwrecked and/
or beaten back each time. None of them reached here.'

'I didn't know that,' Heap said.

'Says the man who is supposed to know everything. If that
means you're fallible like the rest of us, maybe I'll challenge
you to a game of chess next.'

'I'm extremely fallible, Ms Grace. Is it the same local historian who wrote about the Hassocks Blockade?'

Grace nodded.

'I'm still intrigued by the rest of the money from that robbery.'

Grace was sure her walk turned into a stumble. 'What about
it?' she said slowly.

'I want to get my hands on it.'

You and everyone else, Grace thought but didn't say. 'I wish
I could help.'

'Well, perhaps there is something you've forgotten to tell us.
A something you didn't know you knew kind of thing.'

'I can't think of anything I've forgotten to tell you. I didn't
know the white containers were in my lake. I didn't know
that poor, murdered young man had found them. And I don't
know what he could have done with any money he didn't try
to change at the bank. What's happened about that, by the
way?'

'Money recovered from criminal activity goes into the public
purse.'

'They traced the money then?' Grace said casually.

'No,' Heap said. 'This money is untraceable but because of
the particular, peculiar circumstances, the bank decided it was
legitimate to seize it.'

'So no numbers in sequence and all that stuff in movies.'

'It seems not, so the bank would not be able to trace them
back to the Hassocks robberies.'

'Really? And nobody else has tried to cash any more of it?'
Grace was remaining conversational – she hoped.

'Wouldn't know – the bank is reluctant to share with us
details of anyone who brings in out-of-date currency. It has
strict privacy rules.'

'That seems a bit daft,' Grace said as they walked into the
kitchen and she put the kettle on. 'But that means for all you

know all the money might have been converted before even the young filmmaker found his little stash.'

'It might well,' Heap said. 'You never actually met this film-maker?' Heap said.

'Never,' Grace said. 'But what about the other people who were filming with him down at the lake?'

'Apparently they weren't there when he found the containers. They did say he went down on his own to scout locations and camera angles.'

'And Donald Kermode, my stalker? Didn't you say he was captured on film walking with them?'

'He says he never saw any white containers with or without them and that he'd never seen any before because he didn't swim in that part of the lake.'

Grace got two mugs off the shelf by the cooker. 'You know Kermode wrote to me? Saying he felt bad about stealing my underwear off my washing line and would I like it back?'

'What did you say?'

'Are you kidding? I didn't say anything. You know everybody but me knew he's been bragging about wearing my underwear for years – and now the sicko wants to give it me back. Ugh!'

'I'll send PC Edwards, the local community policeman round. By the terms of the restraining order, Kermode is not supposed to communicate with you in any way.'

'Don't punish him, though, please. Just warn him off.'

'Again.'

Grace shrugged. 'Yes, I know. But in my profession at what *was* my level of *stardom*, you kind of got used to the weirdos, if you'll excuse the technical term.' She put the cafetière of coffee on the kitchen top. 'I'm having coffee actually – sure I can't tempt you?'

'OK then. Black, please.'

'I remembered. I've got a great memory for small things; just not so great about the bigger stuff.'

Heap smiled but said nothing. He seemed abstracted. Did he suspect her of having the money?

Grace said, 'But if you don't know whether or not the rest of the money has been converted, why are you still looking for it?'

'I can't see who could have got the money and taken it to the bank – unless, as you say, the rest of it was found before the money the filmmaker found, of course.'

'Of course,' Grace said. 'By the way, how's Kate, your partner?'

Heap looked out of the window. 'That spotted woodpecker prefers those fatballs you've hung out on that branch to the tree it should be drilling into.'

Grace smiled at him. She was fond of this gently know-it-all copper, who wasn't as shy as he might appear when it really mattered. 'Kate?'

Heap smiled breezily. 'Away on a writing course. She wants to write a novel. She's in the old house of Sylvia Plath and Ted Hughes – it's been a writing retreat for years.'

'In Heptonstall?'

'The village is called something like that. You know it?'

'It's near Hebden Bridge and not too far from Haworth. I did a couple of days on a terrible film version of *Wuthering Heights* up there. God, the film was dire but a place called Hardcastle Crags was stunning.'

Heap frowned. 'I missed that film.'

'Lucky you. I'm not even sure it got released over here. It was an international coproduction – i.e. a mess. We filmed most of it in Hungary.' She twitched her nose. 'They paid me well, so I shouldn't complain. But I took the part because my character was married to Albert Finney and I'd always wanted to work with him.'

'How was that?'

'Movie magic.' She laughed. 'But not in the way you think. I was in Hungary filming my scenes with him but he wasn't with me. His half of our scenes were filmed in Yorkshire and I wasn't with him there either. I never actually met him. I spoke all my lines to the second AD – Assistant Director – behind the camera and I guess Albert did the same.' She shook her head. 'I look back at some of the films like that I've done . . .' She gave an exaggerated shudder. 'Ugh.'

'Maybe focus on all the great stuff you've done,' Heap said.

She beamed at him. 'My Sir Galahad,' she said softly. 'So Kate wants to write a novel, eh?'

'Kate doesn't know what she wants to do. The Channel swim was part of that.'

'She didn't make it, did she?'

'Not for want of trying. The pilot insisted we turn back before we reached France. The weather conditions were terrible. So now she doesn't know what challenge to go for next.'

'Why does she need a challenge?'

'Don't we all?' Heap said.

Grace smiled. 'I suppose.' She handed him his coffee and sipped hers. She moved over to her stereo set-up and turned it on.

'*Veedon Fleece*,' Heap said.

'Yes, you know it?' Grace said. 'I would have thought you're the wrong generation.'

'I'm not exactly typical of my generation,' Heap said.

Grace smiled. 'I'm not sure you're typical in any way – which is a good thing, I hasten to add.'

'He made up the term – Veedon Fleece, I mean,' Heap said. 'Van Morrison. It sounds like a mythological thing, a bit like the Golden Fleece – you know, Jason and the Argonauts heading off to get it because it represents kingship and authority? But I guess the Veedon Fleece is meant to be like the Holy Grail – something to search for that will transform our lives.'

'Sounds like we're back to sheep, DS Heap. But, if I may say so I've never known you talk so much.'

Heap flushed. 'Sorry.'

Grace waved her hands. 'No, no, don't apologize. I like it. You're a bright man. A cultured copper.' She wrinkled her nose again. 'I met Van Morrison. Just the once. He was performing *Astral Weeks* live at the Hollywood Bowl ten or twelve years ago. I was just about to leave Hollywood for good, but I went along and ended up backstage; inevitably, I guess.'

'How was he?' Heap asked.

'Taciturn. That's it really – I don't have any big story to tell. Sometimes it's not good to meet people you admire. Back in the day, I could meet anyone I wanted but it always went askew. We've all got feet of clay. That's the reality.'

'If I may say, Ms Grace, I'm very pleased to have met you.'

Grace smiled gently, almost sadly. 'Which is why you're my Sir Galahad. But I too have feet of clay.'

'I doubt that,' Heap said earnestly.

Grace looked away. 'Don't be so sure,' she murmured.

'What do you mean?'

Grace did her big grin but it wasn't quite there. 'Nothing. I'm being silly.' She pointed at a bottle of wine on top of the fridge. 'I drink too much.'

Heap smiled back but didn't say anything.

'My Veedon Fleece would be freedom from myself, I suppose,' Grace continued, 'from the things that bind me because of my nature. I've made so many wilfully stupid decisions in my life because I wouldn't be told – I never will be told! I know best. Except a part of me – an increasingly big part – knows that I don't know best. In fact, I know bugger all.'

'I think that's a common thing,' Heap said.

'Don't tell me that, Bellamy. I don't want to be common! I want to believe that it's unique to me – that I am unique.'

Heap nodded solemnly. 'You are certainly that, Ms Grace.'

'Just fuck right off.'

'I get that a lot.'

'Yeah, well. You must have figured out why, then?'

'Sort of.' Heap gestured towards the chess set. 'I'd enjoy that game of chess with you some time.'

'So you can trounce me? Sure. I love being beaten. And not like that, if you have a filthy mind.'

'I'm sure you're far better than me,' Heap stammered, face red. 'But I'd still like to play.'

'Play what?' Sarah Gilchrist said through the open window.

Grace turned and smiled. 'Door's open, Sarah, come in.'

Gilchrist entered the room and saw Bellamy's bright red face.

'Sarah,' Grace said, grinning that grin, 'Bellamy was offering to trounce me at chess sometime.' She looked at her watch. 'Coffee or a proper drink?'

'Coffee, black, please.' Gilchrist smiled at Heap, wondering why he was red-faced. Had she interrupted something? Surely not?

'I believe you're going to have me transported for stealing sheep.'

'Or hung,' Heap said. 'You know the expression you might as well be hung for a lamb as a sheep?'

'Or is it the other way round?' Grace said. 'A sheep is much bigger.'

'But the meat isn't as tender,' Heap said.

'School's out now?' Gilchrist said with a smile. 'Some fifty sheep and lambs have been butchered – in the proper sense – in the field next door in the past week. Some poachers who know what they're doing have come in, slaughtered the lambs, butchered the meat and left the carcases to rot. Aside from the horribleness of it, it has cost the sheep owner who leases the field a fortune.'

'He's horrible himself though,' Grace said. 'I hear him bellowing at his sheep and his dog really angrily. The guy needs to go on an anger management course. I've seen *One Man and His Dog* – good shepherds do it by whistles and never raising their voices.'

'These poachers certainly took that approach, as they did it in the middle of the night without anybody noticing.'

'Well, I certainly didn't notice.'

'No vans parked on your drive at odd hours? I notice your security gate isn't operational at the moment.'

'I keep forgetting to get it fixed,' Grace said, holding back the fact she couldn't afford it. 'But no, nothing, and I'm sure I would have heard – I'm a bit paranoid about people coming near the house, as you know.'

'When we checked, this gang have been pulling this stunt all over Sussex. They even nicked farmers' sheepdogs to use them to round up the sheep they're stealing. One farmer only twigged when his dog suddenly reappeared after weeks away, but started rounding up his sheep in the middle of the night.'

Grace shrugged. 'I can't help I'm afraid.'

Gilchrist sipped the hot coffee. 'There's something else,' she said.

Grace stiffened, taking a sip of her own coffee.

'We need your help with Billie Grahame,' Gilchrist said.

Grace heard herself expel a long breath but her two police friends didn't seem to notice. 'How can I help with her?'

'We need to talk to her in a more relaxed setting,' Gilchrist said.

'You think she's hiding something?'

'Not intentionally and not hiding really. But we think there might be something she doesn't know she knows. You know she can be a bit vague?'

'There's a lot of that "she doesn't know she knows" around at the moment,' Grace said, smiling at Heap. 'She certainly can be vague, but I sometimes think it's just a performance to get away with stuff and that she's cuter about things than she lets on.' Grace thought for a moment. 'What day is it today? Monday? What about tonight? It's Billie's night off.'

'A Monday?' Heap said, looking puzzled. 'That's unusual in the theatre, isn't it?'

'Very unusual but not unheard of. Until Equity put its foot down back in the day it was quite common for actors to do a Sunday afternoon matinee – two until five – because the theatres did well from the day of rest. Actors and crew then got Sunday evening and Monday evening off.'

'Sounds quite a good deal,' Heap said.

'I would have thought so too, Bellamy, but then I don't have a family. Actors who did were complaining they didn't get their Sunday with the family – Sundays were sacrosanct back then for workers – and Monday their kids were back at school, partners at work, etc. So Equity made the deal. I believe in Australia they still do Sunday matinees with Sunday night and Monday off.'

'That would be great,' Gilchrist said, then looked at her watch. 'But isn't it cutting it a bit tight?'

'She's staying in Guildford while the play is on at the Yvonne Arnaud. She phoned me last night to say she was bored out of her skull at her hotel there.' Grace put on a strange warbly voice. 'All things considered, she said, she'd rather be in Philadelphia.'

'W.C. Fields,' Heap said delightedly. 'That was really good.'

Grace did a little mock-bow. 'Thank you, kind sir.'

Gilchrist looked on, bemused. 'And Bob Watts?' she suddenly said – she didn't know why she said that, but then she didn't know what was going on with her emotionally.

Grace frowned. 'I don't think so – unless you'd like him to come. Are you two back on again?'

'We were never *on*,' Gilchrist said quickly, glancing at Heap.

'Sorry,' Grace said.

Gilchrist felt embarrassed for her little outburst so she grabbed the first thing she could think of: 'Has Bellamy been boring you with his obsession with the Hassocks Blockade money?'

'He mentioned it in passing,' Grace said.

'It's not an obsession per se,' Heap protested. 'It's just the rest of the money from those white containers has not been located. That poor film student only tried to convert a part of it. I'm just curious what happened to the rest.' He shrugged. 'But, as Nimue has just been pointing out, it may be the money has already been cashed in and we wouldn't know because of bank rules.'

'And if it hasn't?' Grace said brightly, perhaps too brightly. 'Where do you think the rest of the money is?'

'It may be stashed somewhere in your wood, I suppose.'

'Feel free to look,' Grace said. 'Have a swim while you're at it, but watch out for the swan coming out of the sun-scald.'

'Sun-scald?' Heap said.

'Old Sussex term for a patch of bright sunlight on water,' Grace explained.

'I'll remember that,' Heap said. 'Isn't it nice to have a swan on your lake along with the ducks?' Heap said.

'Well, it would be if it weren't such a vicious bugger. It attacked me the last time I went for a swim and it attacked me when I was in the rowing boat I stash down there.'

'We saw the swan,' Gilchrist said. 'It did look angry.'

'It would be protecting the nest with the baby swans in,' Heap said.

'Well, yes, I know the male and the cob look after the cygnets together for their first year – although the chicks actually only stay in the nest for one day after they have hatched. But there are no cobs and no cygnets. The swan is alone on the lake, which is probably why he's so angry. He's randy. But I'm certainly not going for any Leda and the Swan scenario.'

Heap smiled appreciatively; Gilchrist kept her ignorance quiet.

'Talk to the Queen – they all belong to her, don't they?' Gilchrist said.

'Oh, that will help!' Grace said with a laugh. 'No, I'm going to have to pay to get him moved somewhere else. I think somebody dumped him on my lake to get him away from their own lake and the disruption he would have been causing there.'

'A combative swan,' Heap said.

'You get them from time to time. Back around 2010, there was one in Cambridge they nicknamed Mr Asbo because he attacked rowers and swimmers. After two years of this, he was moved sixty miles from Cambridge to a secret location.'

'How long does a swan live?' Gilchrist said.

'If he's in tranquil conditions, like my lake, up to thirty years. Did you see the terrapins too? Same thing, somebody dumped them. I need to sneak them over to the pond in Ditchling where the guy who owns it put some in, despite complaints. These ones can go and fight it out with them. They eat newly hatched ducklings, which will play havoc with the breeding programme for the lake.

'I can't let people get away with using my lake as a dumping ground for creatures they're having problems with. Give them an inch and they will take an ell.'

'An ell?' Gilchrist said. 'Do you mean a mile?'

Grace grinned that famous grin. 'Don't you know what an ell is? I didn't either. I had to look it up when I heard someone say it in an old British black-and-white film – *Once In A Blue Moon* – do you know it?'

'I don't but I know the expression as *and they will take a mile,*' Gilchrist said.

'So did I until I saw this film. But a mile seems a bit far don't you think? Anyway, an *ell* is the distance between the tip of your middle finger and your elbow – the length of your forearm essentially. I researched it. It was a common measurement in the Middle Ages – there were even double-ells. Importers of Dutch cloth bought cloth and tapestries by the Flemish ell and sold linen by the English ell.' Grace grinned again. 'I'm trying to turn back time – like all actresses but, in my case, without the plastic surgery.'

'It's used for rope length in *Lord of The Rings*,' Heap said. 'It's the width of the Green Knight's axe head in *Sir Gawain and the Green Knight*.'

Grace looked gleeful. 'My Sir Galahad, you do know your Arthurian legends!'

'Sometimes I think you need a degree just to be around Bellamy,' Gilchrist said. 'Actually, the College of Policing has demanded that all police officers have a degree – so I would never have been able to join the force.'

'When did you join the force?' Grace asked.

'From school. I was sporty not brainy and I wanted an active job.'

'You're very brainy, ma'am, if I may say,' Heap said. 'And if I may further say, so many people confuse *knowledge* with *intelligence*. Just because somebody does well in the pub quiz or on *Mastermind* doesn't mean they're bright. It means they know a lot. And often what they know are undigested facts, learned by rote. It's what you do with that knowledge that matters.'

'You mean you're not brainy, Bellamy? You just know a lot?'

Heap put on an oddly impish expression Gilchrist had never seen before. 'I'm both, ma'am.'

'You cocky bugger!' Gilchrist said.

Heap flushed, of course. 'My tutor used to say that "history teaches you to think" and I think that's true. Studying history makes you a bit of a sceptic, because you don't take the historical record at face value. You have to recognize that the person writing whatever source you're reading has an agenda.'

'This was at the College of Policing?' Gilchrist said.

'I rather telescoped things when I told you I studied the Arthurian Legends at the College of Policing. They sent me off for a year to university, which is where I did various history courses, including that one.'

'Which university?' Grace asked.

'Oxford, Ms Grace. And, as I was saying, my tutor taught me to weigh up competing accounts of the same events by different historians or witnesses and figure out for myself what, on balance, actually happened. Which is pretty good grounding for policework.' Heap turned to Gilchrist. 'Whereas DI Gilchrist didn't need to be taught that. She knew it automatically or learned it on the job or a little bit of both.'

'That's very flattering of you, Bellamy,' Gilchrist said, touched. 'But I'm not sure any of that is true. I just stumble around usually.' Which *was* true. She recognized that without Bellamy she'd

probably never get anywhere. 'And quite often, in the more complicated cases, like this one, the answer lies in the past not the
present.'

'So we beat on, boats against the current, borne back cease-
lessly into the past,' Grace said.

Gilchrist started. 'Scott Fitzgerald.'

'So you *do* know somebody,' Grace said, grinning that grin.

'It came up in a case not so long ago,' Gilchrist said.

'*The Great Gatsby*'s last line came up in a criminal case
around here? How delicious. Do dish.'

'Oh, just a multiple murder case involving Channel Swimmers,'
Gilchrist said.

Grace tilted her head. 'Wow. I can see I need to keep an eye
on you, Sarah Gilchrist. You don't say much – largely because
you make this self-deprecating claim you don't know anything
or anybody – but when you do . . .'

Gilchrist frowned. 'I don't know what you mean.'

'You just delivered the perfect pitch for a movie, twenty-five
words or less.'

'I'm not quite with you,' Gilchrist said. 'As usual.'

'That voyeuristic pervert Robert Altman made this film
called *The Player* about a Hollywood producer, played by
weirdo Tim Robbins, getting away with both murder and the
beautiful female lead of the film – played by the actress who
taught me how to play chess, by the by.'

'She was in *White Mischief*,' Gilchrist said.

'You're on a roll now, aren't you?' Grace said. 'Yes, she
was. Anyway, *The Player* is all about Hollywood really and
these writers and directors are forever trying to get funding
from the Tim Robbins character for their projects and he
insists they explain the project in "twenty-five words or less".'

'And that's what I did?' Gilchrist said.

Heap had quietly left the room.

'Absolutely. But enough of that guff. We're alone for the
moment: I want to know about you, Sarah.'

'What about me?'

'Oh, not your thing with Ostrich Man – though I hope that's
going well, if you want it to.'

'How many ostrich egg omelettes can one woman consume?'

Gilchrist said, and they both burst out laughing though Gilchrist felt guilty that she was betraying Mark Harrison. 'It's over.'

'No – go on, what about your family?'

'Another time about all that.'

Grace looked at her sardonically. 'Barriers, Sarah. Barriers.'

There was the sound of a toilet flushing and Heap came back in. Gilchrist got up to go. There was a thudding against the wall behind Gilchrist. She frowned at Grace.

'An ex I walled up when I got bored with him,' Grace said, po-faced. She laughed. 'Not really. Scared me to bits the first time I heard it. I'd just moved in, alone, in the middle of nowhere, and I heard it when I was in bed. I thought someone was coming up the stairs. It took me a while to realize it was the horses getting restless in what, at the time, were stables next door. They give a little kick against the back wall of their stable – which is the party wall to this place. It's only single skin. I found the sound quite comforting, although I hardly ever hear it now as it's only a couple of horses these days.'

Gilchrist looked at her watch again. 'We'd better scoot if we're coming back tonight. Thanks so much for helping us out. Do you want me to bring some food at such short notice?'

'Don't be daft. I have enough food for an army round here. I shop imagining I'm going to be having big dinner parties then it ends up in the freezer because I can't be bothered and, when I think about it, I don't know enough people to hold a big dinner party. I'll get some stuff out of the freezer.'

'What about a car for Ms Grahame? Unmarked, of course.'

'That might make her suspicious, don't you think? But you know, I might invite Bob Watts so she has someone to ogle, so it doesn't seem so much of a set-up – even though he is police too.

'And don't worry about a car. Even though this theatre company doesn't believe in stars – it's just a company of actors – Billie's agent did negotiate a car and driver as part of her contract. And any of the theatres they are touring in, if they have any nous, splash her name in lights at the front of the theatre.'

'Until this evening then,' Gilchrist said.

SIXTEEN

'Where now, ma'am?' Edwards said when they got in the car.

'Back to the station, Brighton side, please, PC Edwards. Thanks for all your help today.'

'My pleasure, ma'am – it's been a more interesting day than most round here.'

Gilchrist looked at Heap. 'We'll go into the office – unless Darren has woken up. When we're on the train, check with Sylvia Wade what Darren's status is.'

Edwards dropped them at Hassocks and within five minutes they were on a train for the short journey to Brighton. Heap phoned Wade and immediately put her on speaker.

'Darren Jones has woken up, ma'am,' Sylvia Wade said.

'Let's get down there, then,' Gilchrist said to Bellamy. 'OK, thanks, Sylvia.'

'Constables,' Heap said with a nod as they reached the ward Darren Jones was staying in.

'Sir; ma'am,' Constable McGregor said. 'The mother isn't here at the moment.'

'Has she been since he woke up?'

'Negative, ma'am,' McGregor said.

'Hello, Darren,' Gilchrist said heartily, taking one side of the bed while Heap took the other.

Jones looked from one to the other through slit eyes. 'What the fuck do you two fuckers want?' he said sullenly.

'We want to find out who stabbed and nearly killed you,' Heap said.

'Didn't see,' Jones said, closing his eyes. 'Can I get back to sleep now?'

'How could you not see?' Gilchrist said. 'You got stabbed in the chest.'

'He was wearing a helmet, that's how.'

'A crash helmet?' Heap said. 'Can you describe it?'

'Black,' Jones said. 'Can I sleep now?'

'Don't you want us to catch who did this to you?'

'You? You couldn't even catch a fucking cold.'

'Did you have any idea who this person was?'

'Some geezer trying to steal my scooter. Now why don't you fuck off.'

Outside the ward Heap instructed the constables to pin Jones down to a description of the man who assaulted him and get a statement of what exactly happened. They responded enthusiastically.

'Do you think we should try it on again with Pyne, Bellamy? Say Jones has fingered him?'

'Well, we kind of did. We've already got him to give us something big. I think we should chase that up first. Darren is going to keep schtum about being stabbed, so we're not going to be able to press charges.'

'But we don't know where Kobel is, if he's done a runner, do we? Has Sylvia got anywhere?'

'She's working on it, ma'am. We have quite a lot going on though.'

'Tell me about it, Bellamy. Wouldn't it be great if somehow our different cases came together.'

'That kind of congruence only happens in crime fiction, ma'am.'

'*Congruence?* What was wrong with *came together*?'

'Nothing at all, ma'am. Sorry. The fact remains there is no immediately obvious link.'

'Doesn't mean there isn't one,' Gilchrist said stubbornly.

'Indeed.'

Nimue Grace poured Billie Grahame another large vodka from the bottle chilling in an ice bucket by her side. She passed it to her where she lay propped up on the sofa in front of the big log fire.

'Thank you, darling,' Grahame said. 'God, what do we put ourselves through?'

'What do you mean?'

'These agonies.'

'Are you talking as a woman or as an actress, Billie?'

'A woman, of course. I've never found anything agonizing about acting, darling. I just strip off and in sex scenes writhe about and make pretend orgasm noises and spout a few lines.'

Grace smiled. 'You're more than that, Billie, and you know it. You pretend you don't take acting seriously but I know you do.'

Grahame waved the comment away. 'But, yes, I'm talking about us falling for charming narcissists who drag us through the wringer. I mean, is a great shag really worth all the rest?'

Grace shrugged. 'It's never been about the sex for me.'

'Says the woman who had every leading man in Hollywood gagging for her – even the gay ones.'

'That's not quite true,' Grace said, then giggled. 'The gay ones certainly weren't interested even though I tried my luck with enough of them because my gay-meter is non-existent and I didn't realize I was wasting my time. Even then it wasn't about sex. Unfortunately I seemed to find arrogance attractive. When I was younger, I always saw it as self-confidence until it was too late for me to realize the difference.'

'Tell me about it. What about the women?'

'Never interested.'

'Even though you live near Brighton?'

'Even so.'

'I'm pretty sure Cat and Elvira had a thing going on.'

'Did you tell the police?'

'None of my business.'

'They're good people, those two coppers. You should help them if you can.'

'How? I don't know who killed Elvira or where Pinter is. *Theatre-maker* – fuck off!'

'Oh, I don't know, that's not a bad way of describing people putting on those site-specific works.'

'Except this fucking play wasn't specific to anywhere – not even the script it was based on.'

There was a ring on the doorbell. Grace jumped – she'd finally changed the battery, which is all the problem had been, but still wasn't used to the sound. 'That may be those nice coppers now.'

She peered out of the kitchen window that looked over the front door. Sarah Gilchrist and Bellamy Heap were standing there, wine and flowers in hand. Gilchrist caught sight of her in the window and smiled.

Heap had brought a posy of flowers for Billie too. 'Nimue had told us you might be here,' he said, as he offered them to her.

'Well, aren't you an attentive young man,' Grahame said, looking him up and down appreciatively.

'Let me find a little vase for them,' Grace said, taking them from her. 'Bellamy, I'm putting you in charge of drinks while I sort the food. You should know where everything is by now. Although, Billie, you know to help yourself to the vodka.'

As she checked the casserole in the oven, Grace thought back over her phone conversations with Graham Goody and her encounter with William Simpson. She had wanted to hear Bob Watts's view on Simpson, but there was no way she could explain how she knew him without giving the game away.

It was weird: knowing she had this pile of money in the apple cellar was something of a comfort even though it was absolutely no help in paying her bills. Although Bellamy Heap had pretty much said this money could not be traced, she was still nervous about doing anything with it.

Maybe she should leave it there and actually *work* to get out of her financial pickle by re-launching her career. Except the waters closed over so quickly in Hollywood if you stopped swimming with the sharks for even a few months. But her agent was telling her that TV streaming was going through a Golden Age. Netflix, Amazon Prime, Apple, the new Disney+. In fact, her agent had only just called to ask her to come to see her to discuss a potential Netflix series, filming imminently in New Zealand, and another smaller project. Grace was going up to London to see her in the morning.

The doorbell rang again. Bob Watts.

'Ms Grahame,' Heap called as he was sorting out drinks from a table by the piano. 'I gather from Philippa Drake you weren't happy with the fact Cat Pinter kept changing things in rehearsal.'

'Billie. Call me Billie.' Grahame shrugged. 'Absurd woman in that regard. Couldn't make her mind up about anything. Nim, you know—' She looked around. 'Where'd she go? Well, Nim knows what it's like in theatre – even more so in film.' She gave a mock shudder. 'All those takes when a director doesn't know what he wants – and it is usually a he.'

'I worked with one female director – a famous one – who hadn't a clue what she wanted, so the actors pretty much blocked it out for her,' Grace called from the doorway, as she rejoined them.

'Well, actors know what they're doing,' Grahame sniffed.

'Actors *think* they do. They don't always. The film was a disaster.'

'About Cat Pinter . . .' Gilchrist said.

'Dinners are central to this production – the clue is in the title. And my character is a faded Southern belle who dresses for dinner on occasion in her out-of-date Southern belle costumes, albeit now a bit moth-eaten.' She looked at Grace again. 'She is bonkers, this character, you know – very Tennessee Williams – like Amanda in *The Glass Menagerie*? So it was important I got the balance between playing her crazy and making her sympathetic.'

'I'm sure you did it brilliantly, Billie,' Grace almost purred.

'One does one's best, you know. But I was constantly stymied by the changes. You know I learn my lines most efficiently when I associate them with the blocking and the furniture. I say that line here and this line when I move to there and so on.

'So with a couple of chairs and a sofa and a dining table to move to and from and food to serve on the table I was getting my lines right in rehearsal. Then she decided we didn't need the chairs and sofa. We'd stand to have those conversations.

'Then the food went. We were to mime eating. Then the cutlery went so we were to mime using utensils too. Then the candelabra disappeared from the centre of the table so we only had light from the chandelier. Then the dining chairs went so we were to have the imaginary meal using the imaginary cutlery standing around the table at an imaginary fucking buffet. Then the table went . . .'

Grahame sighed theatrically, appropriately enough.

Grace reached out and squeezed her forearm. 'But at least you had your frock.' She saw her look.

'She decided I should wear a fucking tutu instead,' Grahame said. She stretched her legs out in front of her and hitched her skirt up her thighs. 'Fortunately I have good legs, if I do say so myself.'

'We all say it, Billie, because your pins are your best' – she caught Grahame's look – '*one* of your best features.'

'But the arms, Nim! I haven't shown my arms for ten years – nobody my age has good arms.'

'Yours are a miracle of age-defying nature, Billie.'

'Do you think so?' Grahame sniffed, glancing at her arms. 'Well, I suppose they're not so bad.'

Gilchrist had listened to all this both fascinated and impatient. She was waiting for Grahame to drop something inadvertently – or advertently, if there was such a word – Bellamy would know – that would forward their investigation.

'Was anyone else finding it frustrating?' she said.

'Wait just a sec, dear. I haven't finished with my litany of woes. This play is heavily derivative of Tennessee Williams – as I said, think *The Glass Menagerie,* Nimue. So there's a power cut and the candles in the chandelier are lit and the candelabra come into their own although they leave all kinds of deep shadows for things to happen that other characters can't see happening.

'Quite clever, actually – if you have a chandelier and a candelabra. Two days after we lost the candelabra we lost the chandelier too.'

'Where was the lighting source then?' Grace said.

'A match. I had to light a match and pass it to the longshoreman to mime lighting the non-existent chandelier.' She looked at Grace again. 'Lighting a fucking match onstage every night and passing it over without it going out or burning my fingers. I mean, Jesus.'

'At least not as bad as firing a prop gun – or, more usually, not firing it because it wouldn't work.'

'I've been there too, Nim – hence the lines on my raddled old face.'

'You have no lines and you're certainly not raddled.'

'Best you don't see me tomorrow morning, Nim.'

'I'll remember that,' Grace said with a smile, topping up Grahame's glass.

Gilchrist looked. Grace was right: Grahame had no lines, on her forehead at least. But unlike the chief constable her face was still mobile. She should get Grahame to give the chief some tips.

'What did you make of Philippa Drake?' Heap said.

'Who?'

'The stage manager.'

'Oh, was that her name? I make a point of being friendly with the backstage crew but I'm hopeless with names. Didn't really have time to make much of her – she went off on holiday, I think. Only saw her when she got back.'

'Did you ever see her interact with Elvira?' Heap continued.

'*Interact* – there's an interesting word. I occasionally saw Elvira pestering the props master about that fucking Zimmer frame, which, thank God, has gone – along with Cat Pinter apparently. And I saw Cat Pinter and the prop girl *interact*.'

'Did Cat Pinter and the props girl – Flick wasn't it? – have a volatile relationship?' Heap said.

'Oh, I don't know,' Grahame said. She took a gulp of her vodka. 'Actually, I always assumed they got on well. I saw them in quite a huddle one evening – the evening before Cat finally left us alone, actually.' Grahame tilted her head. 'The stage manager was going off on holiday and I assume she was asking Flick to step in. But then the huddle turned into an almighty row. Sotto voce, of course.'

'I think if I were the props girl I'd be pretty cheesed off,' Grace said, 'when things got cut back every day to, essentially, an empty stage with a box of matches and a Zimmer frame.'

'There was the pond at the front of the stage,' Gilchrist said.

'The Hudson River rather than a pond, dear,' Grahame said. 'Yeah, what a stupid, wasteful fucking idea that was.'

'You really don't seem enamoured of this production, Ms Grahame,' Heap said.

'Billie. Call me Billie.'

'He does that,' Grace said.

Grahame put on a Cockney accent. 'I go where the work and the money is, ducks.' She raised her glass. 'And long may there be more of it.'

'Cheers to that,' Grace said, raising her own glass.

After dinner, sitting on sofas and chairs around the log fire, Grace suddenly said: 'My grandfather was light in the loafers.'

Gilchrist and Heap exchanged glances. 'Excuse me?' Heap said. 'I don't know that expression.' Watts shrugged. Nor did he.

'Gay or bisexual?' Grahame rasped.

'Well, bisexual in my grandfather's case. My step-grand-father really, I suppose. Is that what he would be? I'm not sure how these things work. My grandmother had already had my dad by her first husband when Patrick came on the scene.'

'I've never heard that expression: light in the loafers,' Heap said. 'But why do you mention it?'

Grace pointed at a grainy black-and-white photo of herself on the wall behind Billie Grahame. 'Sorry, totally random comment. I hadn't heard the expression either until the photographer who took that photo of me came to do a shoot of me here. Barnaby . . . can't remember his last name. Quite a charmer in that louche English way.' She gestured at the photo. 'And an excellent photographer, don't you think?'

'Any photographer is an excellent photographer when it comes to photographing you,' Grahame said. 'With your bone structure nobody could take a bad photograph.'

'Well, you should talk, Billie.' She looked at the others and gestured at Grahame. 'Terry O'Neill, Bailey, Snowdon all loved her face and did some of the most iconic photos of her.'

'Such naughty boys too,' Grahame said with a throaty chuckle.

Grace smiled and passed Grahame the vodka. 'Anyway, Barnaby – who I suspect was a naughty boy too, but I've never gone anywhere near that with photographers – thought it was a pre-World War Two expression. Although he was using it in reference to a writer he had known. Bruce Chatwin, the late twentieth-century travel writer. Have you heard of him?'

Gilchrist shook her head, thinking, *I've usually never heard of any of the people I'm asked about.*

'What about Patrick Leigh Fermor?' Grace said.

'They don't make them like his type anymore,' Heap said. 'Upper-class adventurer, scholar, poet, travel writer and war hero.' He turned to Gilchrist. 'He was in Crete during World War Two helping the partisans – his account of it, *Ill Met By Moonlight*, was quite a big film in the 1950s.'

'He's the one,' Grace said. 'My step-grandfather knew him quite well before and after the second war. Always referred to him by his initials, PLF. There's mention in an autobiography of Fermor of Gramps going to lunch with him in the thirties with a bunch of happy-go-lucky pre-war souls before PLF set off on a trip to somewhere or other.

'Like Fermor my grandfather was in SOE, part of an odd group of young – and in Gramps' case, not-so-young – men who were called the Small Scale Raiding Force. My grandfather was probably twenty years older than them – he'd served in the First World War so didn't really need to serve again in the Second but he still wanted to do his bit.

'My grandfather's unit went on a small raid in northern France and got clobbered when the boat dropped them off in the wrong place. His skull was smashed to pieces – he was paralysed for a time and needed a steel plate in his skull. He was sent to a prisoner of war camp but was part of a prisoner exchange.'

'What did he do then?' Gilchrist said.

'Briefly he worked for the BBC as a producer, writer, director but his wartime wounds sabotaged him a bit. I suppose he had what these days you'd call PTSD. He never lost his curiosity about things though. He'd met Einstein at some dinner, believe it or not, and got fascinated by quantum physics and, through that, astronomy. I don't know how long that lasted. He had a posh-looking telescope but Dad said he never saw him use it.'

Grace glanced across at Grahame. Grahame had lost interest in the conversation but not the vodka in her nearly empty glass. Grace leaned over and topped her glass up. Grahame gave a bleary smile.

'He liked Victorian poetry. He knew many of the poems by

heart: Arnold's *Dover Beach*, Hopkins' *The Wreck of the Deutschland*, some of *The City of Dreadful Night*. And loads of Tennyson, of course. I've got a lovely copy of *Idylls of the King* passed down to me – well, you saw it on your first visit, Bellamy.'

'Very beautiful it is too, Ms Grace.'

'I also got his copy of *The Complete Works of Shakespeare*, which is what got me inspired to act.' She pointed at her bookcase. 'They're all over there.'

Watts leaned forward. 'Your grandfather sounds quite a character.'

'I only met him once and he was pretty gaga by then. My dad said that in some ways he always had been. Also quite camp and very funny. Did I say that his absolute passion was antiques? He specialized in Georgian silver and Irish glass; I'm not sure why. Again, I have a couple of pieces that were passed down to me. Some lovely silver Apostle spoons that just sit in their case. And that vase over there?' Grace pointed rather airily at a bulbous vase high on a stack of shelves. 'He had an antique shop a few miles down the road from here. My dad said he always wished that his brother had taken over the antique shop rather than drink and smoke himself to death. But my uncle is another Grace family story.'

'You sound like you have a lot of them,' Gilchrist said.

Grace said: 'I think my grandparents were part of a tragic generation. I thought I should write a novel about the family. Maybe I will.' Grace wrinkled her nose. 'Anyway, Gramps was offered the job of being the *Antiques Roadshow* front when it first started. Everybody encouraged him, but apparently he turned it down because he thought he might lose it during the show. He was very changeable. He suggested that avuncular guy whose name I forget should do it.'

Gilchrist shrugged and gave a little shake of her head. 'No idea.' Again.

Bob Watts leaned forward again. 'I wonder if your step-grandfather might also have known my father.'

'Are you that old, Bob?'

Watts smiled. 'Perhaps older than you think. In any event, my father knew Fermor too, before, during and after the Second World War.'

'In what capacity did your father know him?'

'Friend, comrade-in-arms, fellow writer.'

'He was a travel writer too?'

'Crime writer. Pretty successful. I feel sheepish telling you that my lifestyle these days is based not on the sweat of my brow but on his royalties.'

Grace frowned. 'A crime writer called Watts . . .' She unfolded from her chair with such elegance Watts almost applauded. She went over to a bookshelf and, on graceful tiptoe, reached up and pulled down half a dozen books. As she brought them back to him, he recognized the cover of the top one in her pile.

'This is your dad?' she said.

Watts nodded as she proffered him the books and opened the flyleaf of the top one. 'Inscribed to your step-grandfather by my father,' he said.

'They all are,' Grace said. 'What a small world it is.'

'It almost makes us family,' Watts said.

'Oh, I do hope not,' Grace murmured, low enough so the rest wouldn't hear, an impish grin on her face.

Gilchrist was getting bored with all this talk that went way over her head. She was on coffee by now. She put her coffee cup down. 'Bellamy and I should probably be going, Nimue.'

'I need to turn in too,' Grace said. 'I'm going up to London tomorrow to see my agent – and you always have to look your best for your agent, don't you, Billie?'

'You always have to look your best period, darling, when you're a movie star. I'm from the Joan Crawford school – minus the coat hangers and adopted children. She never opened her front door without wearing the full slap and couture clothes.' Grahame touched her face. 'Nor do I.'

'Are you seeing your agent about work?' Gilchrist said.

Grace smiled. 'I'm not sure what I do qualifies as work, despite what some of my more pretentious colleagues might say. But, yes. Something is stirring. I'm not sure what. She was very excited about something that has been offered to me.'

'Bitch,' Grahame muttered.

'Billie! You're doing OK.'

'I'm doing a crap play for *theatre* money, for goodness' sake. That is not my definition of doing OK.' She drained her glass.

'This agent is the American lady we met once?' Gilchrist said.

Grace turned surprisingly steely. 'She doesn't represent me anymore. I don't know what was going on behind my back between her and George Bosanquet, but it just wasn't on. Your agent is meant to look out for your interests but also be your confidante.'

'If you're lucky,' Grahame said. 'Do dish on your Yank agent and Gorgeous George. That creep tried to pick up my sister at a Toronto Film Festival party years ago and it was *hilarious* to watch. Then three years later, he tried to pick me up at a bar in a hotel in Jamaica with about three pounds of blow stuck to his nose. He was repugnant.' She glanced at Grace then into her empty glass. 'Sorry, I probably shouldn't be saying that to you. You were in love with him, weren't you?'

Grahame didn't see the filthy look Grace gave her. She was still looking into her empty glass, presumably to see if somehow she had missed some vodka. Grace leaned over with the bottle and filled her up again. She left the bottle beside the glass. 'We can dish another time,' she said. Turning back to Gilchrist she said: 'No, this is my English agent.'

'I'm sorry to hear that about your American one,' Gilchrist said quietly.

'I'm not. Aside from anything else she was always trying to get me to sign up for a kiss-and-tell autobiography. Publishers were offering a fortune for it but I was always very snooty about it. Well, not necessarily snooty, but I didn't do anywhere near as much kissing as people seem to think and those few I did kiss I certainly don't intend to tell about. So it's never going to happen.' She sipped her wine. 'But a novel, I can see myself writing a novel. Well, in theory.'

'I wouldn't dare write an autobiography about how it has really been.' Grahame said. 'Too many people who might sue.' She put her glass down – a rare occurrence this evening. 'Although I guess Prince Andrew isn't really in a position to . . .'

Gilchrist let that go. She stood. 'I really must be going.'

Heap followed suit and said: 'Me too.' Looking at Grace he cleared his throat and said in an oddly heightened voice: '"Into the face of the young man there had crept a look of furtive shame, the shifty hangdog look which announces that an Englishman is about to speak French."'

Watts laughed and Grahame looked up at him with a bewildered expression on her face.

'Wodehouse!' Grace exclaimed. 'I love Wodehouse.' She gestured vaguely at the bookshelves on the opposite wall. 'I picked up a complete set of his novels in that great second-hand bookshop in Lewes – the higgledy-piggledy one?'

Heap nodded. 'I saw them on your shelves. That's why I quoted him.' He gave a little nod. 'And so that I could say *au revoir*, Mademoiselle Grace.' He turned to Billie Grahame. 'And to you, Mademoiselle Grahame.'

'You're going before it's my turn to go centre stage?' Grahame said in what might have been mock-outrage – but probably not.

'I thought you had been,' Heap muttered. Gilchrist and Grace heard and hid their smiles, but Grahame was focused on her drink and herself.

Gilchrist sat down again. 'No, of course not. How is the production going?'

Grahame took a moment to be mollified, waiting until Heap too sat down. 'Well, as I was saying to Nim, it's been a lot better. The new Vincent actor is pretty good, though sadly gay.' She looked at Grace. 'He's gorgeous.'

'Billie, all the gorgeous ones usually are gay, you know that.'

'True.'

'How's Elvira's replacement working out?' Grace said.

'Flick? She's in her own world but not quite as bad as Elvira was. She's doing a good job.'

'Flick?' Heap said.

Grahame looked over at him. 'Flick, yes? There's a problem with that?'

Heap flushed. 'Not at all. I just hadn't heard the name until recently and now I've heard it twice. We were just talking about the props girl in Brighton who was called Flick.'

Grahame arched her back. 'That's because it's the same person. Flick took over Elvira's part.'

'Was she her understudy?' Gilchrist said, pleased she even knew the word.

Grahame gave a kind of ladylike snort, which was undercut by her saying: 'Understudy, my arse. There was no budget for that in this production.'

'Is that normal then, a backstage person going onstage?' she said.

'Well, of course it isn't normal,' Grahame sniffed. 'But then the circumstances for replacing Elvira are totally abnormal. But backstage staff are often actresses or directors paying their dues until they get a break. And I suppose Flick had seen the rehearsals and the show enough to absorb at least some of the lines.'

'Do you remember Tamara told us she worked as a props girl thing to make her way?' Grace said.

'Well, yes, darling, but she shagged a lot of directors too.'

'I didn't know that,' Grace said, sounding rather prim.

'*Darling*, but you know that happens.' Grahame drained her glass for the umpteenth time. 'We both know a number of actresses whose careers are entirely dependent on the high-profile director they shagged or, more wisely, shagged then married so they would be cast in their big productions. It works in theatre, works in film and telly.'

'You're probably right,' Grace said. 'The way of the showbiz world, I guess, for a hundred and fifty years. The Ziegfeld Follies girls usually had to sleep with Ziegfeld as part of their job description, but they apparently didn't mind if it meant they got onstage. Let's not go into the fact they were all between thirteen and fifteen.'

'Is Flick any good in the part?' Gilchrist said.

'She couldn't be any worse than Elvira,' Grahame said, pouring herself another full glass of vodka. She caught Gilchrist's look. 'I've got hollow legs when it comes to vodka. I can drink it all day and all night and not get a hangover. Sadly, the same can't be said of cocktails. What's that Dorothy Parker little poem? "I like to have a martini, two at the very most, after

three I'm under the table, after four I'm under my host.'"
Grahame looked ostentatiously around, her eyes lingering on
Bob Watts, who had been keeping quiet on a chair in the corner.
'Sadly, a host appears to be in short supply here.' She raised
her glass. 'Hence the vodka.'

Heap said casually, 'Do you mind my asking, Billie, did you
notice any particular intimacy between Cat Pinter and Flick
Steadman?'

'Before, you mean, when she was still props girl?' Grahame
drained her glass. 'I thought we'd talked about that. But OK.
Well, we're all a bit hands-on in our profession. But there was
definitely no touchy-feely once Pinter started going minimalist
and chucking out props. That totally cheesed Flick off.

'I like Flick though,' Grahame continued, 'whatever the short-
comings of her acting. And who cares about her acting in this
crap production? I mean, really? I don't think I told you this,
Nim, but I got the most insulting offer from an ad agency
recently.'

'What?' Grace said, glancing over at Bob Watts, to make
sure he wasn't totally zoned out from all this showbiz talk. He
smiled at her.

'This relates to Flick,' Grahame said, glancing at Gilchrist
and Heap. 'Now it was great money. And I know Harvey Keitel
and Kevin Bacon have both lost their credibility by doing ads
in the UK. Harvey Keitel! Can you believe it? Can he possibly
need the money? You hope they are giving the money to charity.
Anyway, me, I do need the money. But they wanted me to
advertise incontinence pads for the older person. Excuse me,
but fuck right off!'

'Quite right,' Grace said, grinning. 'Or rather: quite wrong.
On so many levels.'

Grahame looked over at Gilchrist and Heap, who both smiled
appreciatively at the story.

'I told Flick,' Grahame continued, 'and she said the last thing
she'd done was an ad for constipation among young women.
You know, that before and after thing. Before is where you act
miserable and suffering. After is when you grin like a loon and
skip across green pastures. We bonded over adverts.' She looked
into her empty glass. 'I mean she's just starting out and needs

whatever work she can get but even so that's going to come back and bite her if she becomes more successful . . .'

Gilchrist and Heap left soon after, Gilchrist determined to make no judgement on the fact Bob Watts was still at Nimue Grace's house.

SEVENTEEN

Bob Watts was, as usual in the mornings after his run along the prom, on his balcony having a coffee. His phone rang. Jimmy Tingley.

'Finally,' he said. 'Should I ask where you are?'

'Canada.'

'Jimmy, I thought we talked about that.'

'We did.'

'What have you done?'

'Nothing you're imagining. I just got a call. Woman called Danvers.'

'Danvers?' Watts laughed. 'Scary, isn't she?'

'She's called you too, eh?'

'Certainly has. Does that mean she's got a job for you?'

'Certainly has.'

'You're gonna take it?'

'Thinking about it.'

'What was the deal?'

'That I didn't do anything bad in Canada.'

Watts grinned. 'Uh-oh.'

Tingley laughed. 'I didn't, I didn't.'

'How long have you been there?' Watts asked.

'About three weeks.'

'What – and you have behaved?'

'They have very good rum here and, because of the French, peppermint is in ample supply.'

'You're in Quebec?'

'Montreal – my new world centre for rum and pep.'

Watts laughed. 'But aside from drinking, what have you been doing?'

'The jazz festival. They have a *great* jazz festival here. Outdoors for free; indoors, the big names. I have been having a very mellow time.'

'That's great to hear – more importantly, to hear that you're safe. When are you back?'

'That depends on whether I take this job.'

'They've offered me a job too.'

'Danvers?'

'Yup. Backroom. Strategic stuff.'

Tingley laughed.

'Why are you laughing?' Watts said, draining his coffee cup and reaching for his cafetière.

'I'm sorry to say this but I'm not sure you're much of a strategic thinker.'

'Thanks very much.'

'Oh, come on, Bob. Do you remember what your commanding officer said? I was there when he said it.'

'What did he say?'

'He said: "faced with an outbreak of malaria you'd start by swatting mosquitos rather than by draining the swamp."'

'Ha ha. And you'd drain the swamp.'

'Well, of course.'

'I consult, Jimmy. I'd figure it out in a consensual way.'

'Bollocks. You consult like most men consult – you decide what you want to do, go through the motions of consulting then do what you always intended to do.

'On the rare occasions I was in organizations – however tenuously – I used to hate fucking managers who made changes for the sake of making change. You know, people who are just concerned to make their mark. So what do they do? They make changes.'

Watts sighed. 'Just get back here, Jimmy.'

Sarah Gilchrist and Bellamy Heap had been down in Portslade all morning knocking on the doors of people Clive Pyne suggested they contact to move ahead with the county lines drug investigation. None of them were home.

The two police officers had called by Darren Jones in hospital first to see if they could get anything more out of him. But, as Heap said, Jones seemed to have adopted some code of silence he'd probably seen in a gangster film. He wasn't going to give up Clive Pyne or anyone else.

Gilchrist was just thinking about lunch – no surprise there – when Sylvia Wade rang.

'Nothing panning out here yet, Sylvia,' she said.

'Sorry to hear that, ma'am, but I have urgent news. Female found dead in Butcher's Wood. Been dead some time. And, ma'am, Nimue Grace found her.'

'Where is Butcher's Wood?' Gilchrist said. 'I've never heard of it.'

'Up behind Hassocks somewhere, ma'am.'

Gilchrist had put the call on speaker. 'Do we know who she is?' Heap said.

'Not yet – but might it be Cat Pinter, sir?'

'Cause of death?' Gilchrist said.

'Well, her heart was cut out and her face bashed in to be almost unrecognisable, ma'am.'

'Her heart cut out? Is it at the scene?'

'Negative, ma'am.'

'Was it cut out where the body was found?'

'I don't know, ma'am.'

'Bilson not there yet?'

'Exactly, ma'am.'

'Where is Nimue Grace?'

'Back at hers, I assume, ma'am.'

Gilchrist looked at Heap. 'We'll get off at Preston Park. Have someone bring our car there and we'll head straight back.'

Nimue Grace was in her large sitting room curled up under a blanket on the sofa in front of a blazing log fire. There was a bottle of brandy with a large glass, now half-empty, beside it and half a dozen scented candles burning on tables nearby. She had almost stopped shivering and was trying not to think about what she had stumbled on in Butcher's Wood.

But images of the bloody, empty chest cavity and the gory mess where a face had once been kept flashing behind her eyes. She'd been in enough gory films to be familiar with fake horrors like that, but the real thing was totally different. And the stench of the decaying body. She couldn't get it out of her nostrils.

She thought the discovery of the body was having such a dreadful effect on her not just because of the horror of it but because it reminded her of the threats her ex, George Bosanquet, the psychopathic South African actor, used to make about what he was going to do to her.

In fact, when she'd seen the body her first thought had been that he had somehow left the body there as a warning to her that she was next. She thought he must be in the area out for revenge, even though, logically, she knew that was impossible since, for the moment, he was wheelchair-bound after Watts and Tingley had given him what the former had referred to as a 'seeing-to'.

Even so, she carried bad memories with her all the time. Unhappy far off things – who'd written that? And she knew the Scott Fitzgerald quote by heart about always being swept back into the past. No way round that, though she assumed that was the same for everyone. She half sat up to reach for her glass of brandy and take a gulp. She lay back down and closed her eyes, willing the movie behind her eyes to stop.

Watts stood out on his balcony, black coffee in hand. He was thinking about Margaret Lively and how he wanted more of Margaret Lively's company. Maybe much more. He couldn't remember the last time he'd felt like this – but he couldn't remember the last time he'd felt so foolish either.

She was too young for him. But she didn't seem to mind. Indeed, she was going into this relationship with her eyes wide open. And his guilt that he had hoped to use her to get William Simpson had gone, now that he was going to use the resources of the National Crime Agency.

He had decided to take the job he had been offered. He had been finding his police commissioner job stultifying since he couldn't get into the nitty gritty of policing through it. At the NCA he hoped he could really make a difference – well, as long as he didn't get tied up in the bureaucracy.

He looked back into his penthouse. He didn't want to leave here but nor did he like the idea of commuting to London every day, although he hoped that he would at least be allocated an

office in Central London rather than the SE11 site the NCA
gave out as its postal address.

He was pondering this when his phone rang. It was Nimue
Grace.

Bilson was busy at the crime scene by the time Gilchrist and
Heap arrived, as it had taken them some time actually to locate
the wood. DC Wade was also there. The corpse stank but there
was also the smell of something else. Perhaps something
intended to hide the stench. The attempt had failed.

Gilchrist gave Heap a questioning look but he just shook his
head. As she walked towards Bilson he put his hand up, palm
first, to stop her. 'Too early to know anything other than the
obvious,' he called, without looking up. 'Much too early to ask
anything.'

'Can I at least ask what that other smell is?' Not that she
could actually smell it now. Bellamy had told her that smell
was the weakest sense and he was usually right about pretty
much everything.

'That would be camphor. And a lot of it. You may know it
as mothballs.'

Mothballs. Immediately Gilchrist was swept back to an image
of her grandmother, confined to her bed in her old age and
young Sarah opening a drawer to get her grandmother's Bible
and being hit with this smell.

'Bellamy tells me that while our sense of smell is the weakest
on repetition it's the strongest in terms of access to our
memories.'

Bilson didn't look up but said: 'Bellamy has proved himself
to be factually correct yet again. It is particularly acute combined
with our sense of taste – most famously with Proust and his
madeleine.' He looked up now. 'My reference, since I'm
guessing you may not have read Proust, is not to a woman
called Madeleine he knew intimately, but to a biscuit of that
name that evoked a twelve-volume, four-and-a-half-thousand-
page memory novel from him.'

'That's some biscuit,' Gilchrist said.

'It is indeed, Sarah. Now I really do need to get on.'

'When you said the word *mothball* it immediately reminded

me of my grandmother. But this smell didn't. Why would that be.'

Bilson looked up again. 'It may be that the mothballs your grandmother used were mostly naphthalene or paradichloroben-zene – what we have here is pure camphor, often just one of the ingredients in cheaper mothballs.'

'So is it here to disguise the smell of decay?'

'Given there is a camphor ball stuffed in her mouth I'd say probably not. Taken externally it's an antiseptic. Taken intern-ally, camphor kills if taken in sufficient quantities. It causes seizures and then heart failure.' He looked down at the broken body. 'Although there are a plethora of possibilities for cause of death here.'

'And was it taken internally as well as stuffed in her mouth?' Gilchrist said.

'Do give me a chance, beautiful Sarah,' Bilson said. He gestured to the open chest cavity. 'Although I can see the stomach I don't intend to look inside it here.'

'Sorry, Frank,' Gilchrist said. 'I'll let you get on.'

She turned to DC Wade. 'We have no reason to believe this is Cat Pinter but get in touch with Twickenham police and ask them to get DNA from the Pinters just in case.'

'It would be a bit of a stretch, ma'am . . .' Heap said.

'Well, it just seems a bit of an odd coincidence that we have a woman who appears to have disappeared off the face of the earth and we have a murdered woman here. But I'm not assuming it's her by any means.'

'Just hoping it is,' Heap murmured.

Gilchrist ignored that. She looked around. 'Anything of obvious interest here, Sylvia? Handbag? Computer? Phone?' She swallowed. 'Heart?'

'Nothing so far, ma'am,' Wade said. 'Mr Bilson said some-thing in Latin, ma'am, when he said the heart was missing.'

'Shall we leave them to it, ma'am?' Heap said.

Gilchrist nodded. 'Let's go and talk to Nimue Grace. Sylvia, come with us. Call Twickenham on the way.'

'Ma'am.'

She called back to Bilson. 'Frank, what was with the Latin and the missing heart.'

He didn't look up. 'Tuscan Italian, actually. Dante. You can hear a mistranslation and a nice bit of opera about it in the film *Hannibal*.' He looked up. 'About a lover eating your heart.'

'You know the film, *Hannibal*, Bellamy?' Gilchrist asked on the way to Plumpton.

'Good film. The sequel to *Silence of the Lambs*, though thankfully the director didn't go the whole hog with the ending of the novel it's based on. That was very Grand Guignol.'

'Bilson used that phrase – what does it mean?'

'Over-the-top horror, but in a Gothic kind of way not a *Texas Chainsaw Massacre* kind of way.'

'I'm not sure I'm any the wiser but I'll leave that there,' Gilchrist said, 'So Hannibal eats some lover's heart?'

'No he quotes – well, actually, misquotes, as I recall – a part of Dante's famous long poem, *Vita Nova*, which does involve a heart being offered to be eaten. But the scene in the film is set at an opera, especially written for it by Patrick Cassidy, where there is an aria based on the particular sequence of the *Vita Nova* which has the heart eating sequence in it.

'It's beautiful, but because it's sung in Italian most people have no idea what it's saying. Katherine Jenkins had a big hit with it later. Ridley Scott, the director of *Hannibal*, used it again – inappropriately but because it's beautiful, I suppose – in his *The Kingdom of Heaven*. Excellent film in the DVD director's cut by the way. And I think Ridley's brother Tony Scott used it in one of his films, but I can't be sure about that.'

Gilchrist just stared at Heap as all this spilled out of his mouth. 'You say most people don't know what these words mean in the Italian song, but you—'

Heap gave a little shrug and looked out of the car window. 'We're here, ma'am.'

Nimue Grace was sitting on her sofa in front of a log fire when Gilchrist, Heap and Sylvia Wade arrived at her French windows. She had a blanket over her shoulders, a glass of brandy in her hand and Bob Watts sitting, rather stiffly, beside her.

Grace looked startled when she saw them at the window.

After a moment, she beckoned them in. Gilchrist looked at Watts, popping up yet again. 'Hello, Bob.'

Watts nodded and stood. 'You'll be wanting to talk to Ms Grace about her grisly find, so I'll get out of your way.'

'Please stay, Bob, since you've come all this way,' Grace said. She looked at Gilchrist and Heap. 'I hope that's OK.'

Gilchrist nodded. 'Fine with us. We just wanted to talk to you about the circumstances of your discovery.'

Grace gestured to the other sofa. 'Sit, please.' She looked at Watts. 'And, Bob, please stop hovering. Or go to the kitchen and get everyone a drink.' She looked back to Gilchrist and Heap as they perched at the front of the other sofa. Sylvia Wade had taken a chair in the corner. 'Billie went back to Guildford this morning – how anyone can be so fresh in the morning after downing a couple of bottles of vodka I have no idea. Anyway, I didn't want to be alone and I didn't know who else to phone so I called Bob.'

'Understandable,' Gilchrist said, as Watts went off down the corridor.

'What were you doing in the wood, Ms Grace?' Heap said.

'Nimue, for frick's sake!'

The flush on his face predictably came. 'The question remains the same, ma'am.'

Grace sighed. '*Ma'am*? Now you're regressing, Bellamy. I'd been up to London on the train to see my agent about any work that might be on the horizon. Do you remember I said last night? I was coming back from that visit.'

'But your train would come to Plumpton, wouldn't it?' Heap said. 'On the Littlehampton line through Lewes?'

'Yes, it would. But I was going to visit an old friend in Hassocks, so I took the Brighton line.'

'Why were you in the wood, then, if you were visiting someone in Hassocks?' Heap said, looking puzzled.

'You're being quite the detective this morning, aren't you Bellamy,' Grace said flatly.

'It's work, Nimue. Just best to get the facts clear at the outset.'

Grace gave him a weak smile. 'Well, I say Hassocks, but actually she lives in the country just outside Hassocks. There's a lovely old Elizabethan place called Danny House that has been converted into apartments for older people to retire to. My friend lives in one of those. I thought I would walk there from the station.'

'You've done that walk before?' Heap said.

'Never,' Grace said, taking a sip from her brandy. 'But the map app on my phone was my guide. I almost turned back when I saw this sign that told me I was going to go through a Butcher's Wood. Gave me the shivers.' She shivered now. 'Maybe it was prescience.'

'What happened then?' Gilchrist said gently.

'Well, as I was walking through on this narrow path, I saw this man about a hundred yards along the path coming towards me. Rough-looking guy. I didn't like the thought of being in a secluded place with some stranger. He seemed to be in his own world – ignoring the bluebells and just looking at the ground in front of him – and that worried me more. But I thought he probably hadn't seen me.'

Grace paused for a moment to take another sip of her brandy. 'So I stepped off the path and through some pretty thick undergrowth so I could go round him without him seeing me. I was stepping very carefully so he wouldn't notice me so I was looking at the ground too, probably more intently than I normally would.'

She worked her mouth and swallowed. 'First I saw what now I know was clearly blood spattering the bluebells and wild garlic flowers. And then I saw this *thing*. I went over to it and . . . well, you know what I found.' She took a deep breath. 'Of course, I thought it was something to do with the man I'd seen, so I hid in some bushes. And that's why I couldn't get away from the stink which is still in my nostrils.'

'She'd been dead for some time,' Gilchrist said gently, 'so that man had not just committed that crime.' She looked over at Wade. 'Even so, Sylvia, we can't rule him out. Get PC Edwards to canvass the houses at either end of the wood to see if he lives there or if they know who he is. He probably is innocent, but if he is maybe he saw something if he walks through there regularly.'

'I realized that the person had not just been murdered

when I left the wood later,' Grace continued. 'I could see that the blood and gore was dried but I didn't process it. I wasn't thinking too clearly.'

'Understandably,' Gilchrist said. 'What did you do after you hid in the bushes?'

'Well, I realized it was stupid to hide so near to the body if he was going to come back so I moved further and further away as quietly as I could then I made a run for it.'

'You didn't encounter this man?' Heap said.

'Thankfully not. And once I was out of the wood, I called the police – well, when I could get a signal. The rest you know.'

'Thank you, Nimue,' Gilchrist said. 'Can you think of anything else that might help us?'

Grace thought for a moment. 'Mothballs,' she said. 'Kind of.'

'Yes, I noticed that too. Apparently it was camphor.'

'Was the killer trying to hide the smell? Because that didn't work.'

'Probably not but we're going to explore that,' Gilchrist said.

'Can I ask you a question?' Grace said.

'Of course.'

'What had happened to the chest?'

Gilchrist and Heap exchanged glances. 'The heart had been removed,' Gilchrist finally said.

Grace grimaced. 'Why? Some kind of serial killer trophy thing?'

'We don't know,' Gilchrist said. 'But we don't think this is necessarily some kind of serial killer crime.'

'Have you identified the victim?' Grace said. 'Is it a man or a woman by the way? I couldn't tell from the little look I took.'

'The victim is a woman but, no, we haven't identified her yet. We're hoping fingerprints and DNA will do that for us.' She looked to Heap. 'I don't think we need to bother you any more, Nimue.'

'Well, a description of the man you saw would be useful,' Wade interjected.

'Six foot or so. Skinny. Dressed in baggy jeans and a dark raincoat. Straggly long black greasy hair parted in the middle. Possibly a beard but maybe just hadn't shaved for a bit – I wasn't near enough to see his face properly. Shambled rather than walked, hands in his pockets.' She shrugged. 'That's all I can think of.'

'That's pretty impressive,' Gilchrist said. She looked at Heap. 'Good to go?'

They stood just as Watts came back in without any drinks. 'I was too slow? You're leaving. I should probably go too, Nimue, unless you'd like me to stay.'

Grace smiled weakly. 'If you've got nothing better to do for the next hour.' She stood, a little shakily. 'Goodbye, you three. Are you allowed to keep me informed of the progress of the investigation?'

'We'll tell you what we can,' Gilchrist said, determined not to think about Bob Watts staying here to comfort Nimue Grace.

Sylvia Wade phoned Heap. He put it on speaker. 'A couple of things, sir. DNA shows the body to be that of Cat Pinter. Mr Bilson says she was dead when the heart was removed and that she probably died from ingesting a large number of camphor balls although her injuries would have been a large factor too. I'm quoting. He found the camphor balls in her stomach. Apparently ingesting camphor leads to seizures and heart failure.'

'Thanks, Sylvia. Did he say any more about the possibility of the heart being taken in order to eat it?'

'I did ask, ma'am, but he said that it wasn't his department to assign—'

'—motive. I know that's what he would have said. "That's your job, Sarah. For me it's just the facts," etcetera, etcetera.'

Wade laughed. 'More or less, yes, ma'am.'

'And the other things?'

'Just one really. PC Edwards has come up with a potential witness in one of the cottages at the edge of Butcher's Wood. Woman called Sasha has identified the man Ms Grace saw in the woods, but also saw some unusual activity around the time the body was likely dumped there – not activity by him though.'

'Sasha what?'

'Sasha is all I've got, ma'am.' She gave Heap the address.

'Back over the Downs, ma'am?' Heap said. Gilchrist nodded.

EIGHTEEN

Gilchrist looked Sasha up and down. Somewhere in her twenties, she was enhanced in so many ways she made chief constable Karen Hewitt, who had a Botoxed-to-buggery face, seem like a rank amateur. The stick thin legs were probably hers but nothing else looked real.

'Yes?' Sasha said through plumped-up lips, jerking Gilchrist back into the moment.

'Ms . . .?'

'Sasha.'

'Ms Sasha?'

'Just Sasha.' She looked Gilchrist up and down. 'You're another pig?'

'Pig? Really? In this day and age?'

'You think pig is a sixties hippy expression from America, don't you?' Sasha said with a smirk. 'Well, it's not. I googled it once. It's English and it dates back to the early nineteenth century – around 1811, if I recall. Perfectly acceptable, therefore.'

'Unless you're a policeman, of course, in which case not quite so acceptable. May we come in?'

'Oh – two of you – sorry, Constable, I didn't see you hiding behind this one.'

'Detective Sergeant Heap and *this one* is Detective Inspector Gilchrist and I'd ask you to keep a civil tongue in your head, if you don't want us to take your statement through the bars of a prison cell.'

'Will do, sir,' she said with a smirk. 'And please come in.' She stepped aside and bowed them in. She led them to a room in which pretty much everything was pink.

'You've had a bad time with the police?' Gilchrist said, equably.

'Over the years,' Sasha said, sitting down, and crossing her skinny legs. 'But I'm just cynical of all authority.'

'Then it's very kind of you to help us. What do you do, by the way, Sasha?'

'I'm a social media influencer.'

'I think you might need to expand on that answer,' Gilchrist said.

'Paid or earned?' Heap said. Trust him to know something about it.

'Paid – on Twitter and Instagram. I recommend stuff I've been asked to check out for my followers.'

'How many followers do you have?' Heap said.

'Two hundred and twenty-three thousand at the last count.'

'What kind of products?' Heap said.

'Well, I got a big response promoting Katy Perry's shoes.'

'Katy Perry's shoes?' Gilchrist said. 'A shoe-maker?'

'A massive pop star. She created a collection of food-shaped shoes.'

'You're going to have to walk me through this,' Gilchrist said looking to Heap who could only shrug.

'Katy is a very wise woman. She pointed out that the universe is vast and that you can get inspiration from so many different places in it. Through music, movies, travel – and food.'

'So not really quite all the universe then,' Gilchrist said.

Sasha ignored that. 'Her shoe collection is really about storytelling – with a sense of humour, obviously, to get ideas for new heels. My own favourites were the watermelon slides.'

As so often these days, Gilchrist felt she was living in a parallel world to everybody else. 'How did you come to be in Hassocks, Sasha?'

'Well, the last thing I approved of was a spa weekend near Hurstpierpoint.'

'You stayed for the weekend?' Gilchrist said.

'I stayed for the week as part of my payment. It was a great detox. And I liked it so much I decided to move here.'

'Isn't it a bit of a quiet place for a media influencer?' Heap said.

'Well, you know, Brighton is only fifteen minutes away and London an hour away. And I like quiet places and old pubs – which is how I know Gary.'

'You know we found a body in the woods?' Heap said. 'Do you ever go in there?'

She gestured to her high heels. 'Are you kidding me?'

'But this Gary, the man who regularly walks through the Butcher's Wood. He's a friend?'

'No, he's not even a sesh friend. But I know who he is. He goes past my window pretty much every day.'

'I don't know what one of those is, I'm afraid,' Gilchrist said.

'You don't know what a window is?' Sasha had a really irritating smirk. 'Just kidding. A sesh friend is just somebody who isn't a real friend but you see around and maybe hang out with at the end of a party. But you'd never meet anywhere else.'

'Do you have any real friends?' Gilchrist blurted out, irked by this woman. Just as she was kicking herself, Heap intervened.

'Why *sesh*?' he said.

'I have no idea,' Sasha said, her eyes on Gilchrist. 'Of course I have real friends. Do you want me to tell you what I saw or not?'

'Please,' Gilchrist said meekly – well, meekly for her.

'OK. So, just to finish off about Gary. He was a regular in the pub round the corner that I go to sometimes. Always at the bar. I used to take my laptop in there.'

'You don't seem the pub type,' Gilchrist said.

Sasha gave her another hostile look. 'I don't think of myself as a *type*. What *type* are you?'

'The detective inspector is the police officer type,' Heap said, 'so please go on.' Heap glanced over at Gilchrist and raised a questioning eye at her attitude. Gilchrist knew she was being stupid but couldn't help being incredibly irked by this stupid woman with her twig legs and fake body. An *influencer* for fuck's sake.

'Well, as I said, I don't really know him. He was a regular in the pub. One of that gang who sit at the bar and think they own the place, so it's hard for anyone else to order a drink.'

She recrossed her legs and touched her plumped-up mouth with a long lacquered fingernail. 'Anyway. Enough about him.

On this particular day. I was writing my first tweets of the morning.'

'Roughly what time was this?' Heap said.

'Around five.' She saw his look. 'That surprises you? I was wide awake as I'd just got back from clubbing in Brighton and I had to write about that while it was fresh in the mind. I wasn't going to post them until later in the day, of course.' She clasped her hands over her bony knee. 'Anyway, I'd noticed a woman sitting in a car across the street as I came home. I thought it was a bit odd but that was all.'

'And you can describe this woman?' Heap said.

'Not from that glance, no, but could you just bloody hang on and let me tell this story my way?'

'My apologies, miss,' Heap said. 'Please go on.'

Sasha gestured at the desk in front of the window. 'I do my work there. So I'm sitting there with my laptop and a large vodka' – she turned to Gilchrist and fluttered her long false eye-lashes, almost covering her cheeks in the process – 'does it count as hair of the dog if you've been drinking all night and are just carrying on?'

Gilchrist just gave a little smile.

'I'm distracted by three men in paint-splattered overalls coming past the window from the direction of Butcher's Wood and getting in a car.'

'You'd seen them before?' Heap said.

'Never. They were just your typical builder types – stocky, stubble, shaved heads. But as I said they were just a distraction.'

'And they were coming from the wood?'

'I assume so,' Sasha said impatiently. 'That direction anyway.'

'What colour was the paint?' Heap said.

'What? Can I just tell the rest of my frigging story?'

'Calm down, miss, please,' Heap said.

'Calm down? You want my help and you treat me like some kind of – what's that expression? – *hostile witness*?' She pointed a manicured finger at Gilchrist. 'Especially *her*.'

'Once again my apologies,' Heap said. 'And I'm sure I speak for the detective inspector when I say that.' He glanced at

Gilchrist but she said nothing. He smiled at Sasha. 'Please tell us the rest of your frigging story.'

Sasha waited a moment, nostrils flaring but in a bit of an abnormal way, as far as Gilchrist could tell – a kind of mini-flare. Nose job too, she concluded.

'So, because of the men going by I didn't see the woman get out of the car. But I saw her walking off in the direction of the wood. Then about half an hour later I saw her come back, get back in the car and drive off.'

'What did you find unusual?' Heap said. 'Don't lots of people walk in the woods?'

'At five in the morning? And without a dog?'

'But this time you got a good look at her,' Heap said.

'Yeah. Now I can describe her, if you'd like. Hippy type, hair a long, tangled mess. Blonde. Terrible dress sense like a lot of hippies who think they're being arty.'

'Why terrible?'

'Clashing colours and patterns. Stupid hippy sandals.'

'Birkenstocks?' Heap said.

'No, they were way uglier.'

'What was she wearing aside from the sandals?'

'Baggy chequered pantaloons and a striped smock kind of thing. Oh and she had a big shoulder bag – some tapestry material of course. She was very careful about putting it in her car – went round the passenger side and laid it carefully on the seat. I noticed that.'

'So she took that with her?'

'Obviously from what I've just said.'

'And what did she look like?' Heap said.

'Intense. Not the kind of girl you could have a laugh with. Sort of tight-faced.' Sasha did the lacquered fingernail to the plump mouth thing again. Gilchrist had to look away, resisting the urge to reach over and snap one of her twig legs. *Get a grip, Sarah*, she told herself.

Sasha frowned. Gilchrist was surprised she was still able to do that. 'The thing is, her face was familiar.'

'You've seen her before?'

'Somewhere but I don't know where.'

'The local pub? A Brighton club?'

'No, nothing like that. I don't think I've seen her face to face and certainly not around here. But her face is very familiar.' She shrugged. 'It'll come to me.'

Heap stood and handed over his card. 'For when it does come to you.' Gilchrist stood too. Heap looked at her. 'I think we're done here, Detective Inspector?' She nodded. Heap turned to Sasha, who was already turning her television on. 'Thank you for your time and information, Sasha,' he said to her back.

'Sure,' she said.

Heap pretty much hustled Gilchrist out of the door. But he turned and said: 'Sasha – I forgot, sorry. You never told us the colour of the paint on the overalls.'

Sasha almost smiled. 'I just saw brown but there were probably others.'

'Thank you.' Heap stayed looking at her. 'Sasha, this is an ongoing murder investigation. Please don't tweet or in any other way post about our visit. However, once this is over – the minute it is over, in fact – I promise I will fill you in so you're on the inside track for what used to be called a scoop in the press. I have no idea what the social media equivalent of a scoop is.'

Sasha looked at his card. 'You, I believe.' She gestured to Gilchrist behind him. 'Her I wouldn't trust as far as I could throw her – which wouldn't be far given the size of her.'

'She didn't mean you were fat, ma'am, she just meant you were much bigger than her.'

'It's fine, Bellamy. It's been that kind of case. I'm sorry I lost it in there.'

'Why was that, ma'am? I mean, I know she was irritating but—'

'If I knew that, I wouldn't have been like that, would I?' She looked across at Heap. 'Sorry. There I go again. I don't know what's wrong with me. I was appalling in there. It's just that women like that – I mean look at her! – drive me nuts.'

'I understand, ma'am. Where to now?'

'About the paint on the overalls—'

'Remember blood turns brown when it dries, ma'am.' Heap's phone rang from an unfamiliar number. 'DS Heap.'

'It's Sasha. I've just seen her.'

'On your street?' Heap said.

'On the television. She's the uncomfortable-looking young woman in the constipation ad.'

'Did you know Flick was short for Felicity, Bellamy?' Gilchrist asked, as they stood inside the stage door of the Yvonne Arnaud theatre. Uniformed police were on guard outside the door and at the front of the theatre. They were trying to look inconspicuous. 'Like a tarantula on an angel cake,' Heap had murmured when they first arrived. He saw Gilchrist's look. 'Raymond Chandler, ma'am, describing, if I remember correctly, Moose Molloy.'

'You usually do remember correctly,' Gilchrist said. 'Now even I've heard of Chandler. He's the *Maltese Falcon* guy.'

'Close but no banana, ma'am,' Heap said as they went through the stage door.

Gilchrist was going to ask what *that* meant but the stage door manager, a thin woman in huge horn-rimmed glasses, slid open her window and said quietly, 'The show will come down in about five minutes,' then closed it softly again.

As they were standing there, Heap now said: 'As discussed, I didn't know Flick was short for Felicity, ma'am. I don't think I've ever met a Felicity. I'd vaguely understood Fliss to be a shortened version of it but I've never knowingly met one of those either. Similarly, I only recently discovered Pippa was short for Philippa.'

'I knew about Pippa but never understood why anyone would want to call themselves something that sounds like you've got a weak bladder.'

Heap smiled. 'Let's not even think about the possible foreshortenings of my name or the nicknames it produced at school,' he said.

Gilchrist nodded solemnly. 'Yes, let's not go there.'

Spotlight acting directory had finally come through to Sylvia Wade with a list of Felicitys. There were about twenty of them. Wade had emailed the images through to Olivia Oland, the directors' agent, who had eventually got back identifying Felicity Steadman as the woman who had accompanied Cat

Pinter to one of her soirees. By then, *Spotlight* had come back to Wade with a list of Felicitys with their acting credits, as best they could tell. And there was Felicity 'Flick' Steadman, currently appearing in *The Dinner Game*.

The stage door manager slid open her window again. 'The show has just ended. Do you want me to take you to Miss Grahame's dressing room?'

'Yes, please,' Gilchrist said.

'They're taking their bows,' the woman said, as she led them down a narrow corridor and stopped in front of a door with Billie Grahame's name on it. 'But there aren't usually many for this show.' She gave them a puzzled look. 'Usually Miss Grahame likes to get herself sorted before she sees anybody – aside from anything else, her make-up is a bit garish for this production – but she said I was to let you in to wait for her.'

The dressing room was small and brightly lit. It was cluttered with a single bed covered in throws with a small fridge beside it, an armchair crammed into a corner of the room and a wide, low shelf-cum-desk in front of a mirror with lights all around it. The mirror had various postcards and congratulation cards stuck to it. The shelf was cluttered with more cards, three vases of flowers – two lavish, one not quite so much – two make-up bags, a magnifying mirror on a stand and two buckets of champagne with a dozen glasses beside them. There was a small washroom beyond.

An open wardrobe had, presumably, Billie Grahame's day clothes on hangers and several pairs of shoes underneath.

Grahame burst into the room and smiled, cracking what really was garish make-up. 'The game's afoot, eh, Detective Inspector?' she whispered throatily. She threw herself down on the single bed and reached out an arm. 'Would one of you be a dear and pour me a glass of champers?'

'You look like Theda Barr, if I may say, Ms Grahame,' Heap said, as he cut the foil and then turned the wine key of one of the bottles. 'Lying there like that.'

Grahame eyed him. 'I would normally be surprised that someone your age even knew who Theda Barr was, but Nim told me you know everything about everything.' She looked at Gilchrist. 'That must be a real pain day to day.'

Gilchrist considered saying *tell me about it*, but instead she looked over fondly at Heap. 'No, I quite like it,' she said.

Heap flushed as he opened the champagne expertly without a pop.

'Well, at least he didn't compare me to Mae West, even in this ridiculous make-up. Though if you can find a grape to peel over there, Beulah . . .'

Heap smiled and handed her the glass of champagne. Grahame looked on appreciatively. 'A man who knows how to open the fizz properly. Popping the cork is *so* vulgar. And how to pour it. Why so few people think to tilt the glass, I'll never know. Thank you, my dear. Pour yourselves a glass quickly so we can toast to, well, I don't know what. Deduction?'

'We probably shouldn't,' Heap said.

'Nonsense,' Grahame said. 'You need a glass in your hand for verisimilitude for when she first comes in.' She half leaned towards them. 'Have you any idea what it's like,' she hissed quietly, 'to share a stage with a *murderess*?'

'I'm sure it's a story you'll be able to tell for some time,' Gilchrist said as Heap passed her a glass of champagne.

Grahame kind of leered. 'Don't you worry about that, dear. I've already got that figured out.'

Heap poured himself a half of one. 'To deduction,' Gilchrist said, taking a healthy sip and noticing Heap took a tiny one.

'Pour some more for our guests, will you?' Grahame said.

'Guests?' Gilchrist said. 'We were hoping there would only be one, Ms Grahame.'

Grahame looked towards the closed door. 'Well, I could hardly only invite *that person*, could I?' she breathed. 'That would be suspicious.' She looked from Gilchrist to Heap. 'I see you're nervous about performing in front of an audience. Don't be, just tell yourself the stage is yours.'

There was a tap on the door.

'*Entrez*,' Grahame called.

Flick Steadman walked in, wearing chequered baggy trousers and a striped smock, a big tapestry bag over her shoulder. 'Just for a quickie, Billie,' she said before she clocked Gilchrist and Heap. Her eyes narrowed. 'Hello. I know you, don't I?'

'Sort of,' Gilchrist said, as Heap handed her a glass of champagne.

'You were great tonight, as always, Billie,' she said, taking a sip of her champagne, her eyes still on the policemen. 'But you haven't taken your make-up off yet.' She looked at Gilchrist and Heap. 'Have we barged in too early?'

'I was, wasn't I?' Grahame said. 'But, yes, it exhausted me, so I decided drink before make-up.' She raised her glass. 'Chin, chin.'

Steadman looked at her now. That same intense look. 'I did all right though, didn't I, Billie?'

'Fabulous, darling. Simply fabulous.' Grahame gave her a big smile but even Gilchrist, the least sensitive of people, could see how false it was. So could Steadman. Her attention swivelled back to Gilchrist and Heap. 'What did you think of the show?'

'Didn't see it, I'm afraid,' Gilchrist said.

Steadman took another sip of her drink, her eyes flicking from one to the other of them. 'Why are you here then?'

'Cat Pinter's heart,' Heap said.

The temperature in the room seemed to plummet. Gilchrist could hear the silence. Steadman stared at Heap for a long moment, then took another sip from her champagne. 'You're police?'

Heap and Gilchrist both nodded.

She tilted her head. 'What about her heart?'

'It's missing.'

Steadman touched the side of her bag. 'Not really,' she said quietly.

NINETEEN

Flick Steadman sat upright in the interview room, her hands flat on the table in front of her. Sarah Gilchrist sat opposite her and next to Gilchrist, Bellamy Heap leaned against the wall.

'Why did you cut her heart out?' Gilchrist asked.

'Isn't it obvious?' Steadman said. 'To see if she really loved me.'

'Were you going to eat it?' Heap said.

'Do I look like Hannibal Lecter or some Dante nut? Although that was a wild bit in the film, at the opera when Hannibal recites to the wife of the crooked cop he was about to kill the poem about Dante giving his beating heart to his lover to eat.' She cackled. '"Intestines in or intestines out, inspector whatever-his-name-was?"'

There was a long pause.

'And did she love you?' Gilchrist said.

Steadman's face hardened. 'You see, I thought she couldn't have loved me, because if she had she would never have taken the part away from me.'

'What part?' Gilchrist said. 'The part Elvira Wright had in *The Dinner Game*? What do you mean by taken it away from you? I thought you were the props girl.'

Steadman raised her chin. 'I'm an actress, *darling*. As must be clear by now. Cat gave me the props master gig so she'd have me with her on the tour. And I shouldn't have taken it because she'd just let me down over the part, but I loved her. Loved her so much. With that burning passion – you know it? – that means nothing else matters.' She looked at Gilchrist. 'Do you know it?'

Gilchrist ignored the question, largely because no, she didn't know that feeling. 'So what went wrong?' she said.

Steadman's face hardened again. 'Well, bad enough she took my part away but then she began treating me like a skivvy, disrespecting me, treating me with contempt in front of others. And then she started getting rid of prop after prop. Suddenly demanding a fucking Zimmer frame was almost the last fucking straw.' She clasped her hands. 'But then I realized why she was treating me so badly. Not only had she chosen that Albanian bitch over me for the role she'd promised me, but she'd also chosen her to replace me in her bed.'

Gilchrist and Heap exchanged glances at the words *Albanian bitch*. Gilchrist gave a little shake of her head: they'd get back to that. 'You mentioned contempt – how did that show itself?'

'Well, here's an actress demoted to props girl. It usually works the other way round. You work as a skivvy until you get your break.'

'And this play was your break?'

'Yes, and I gave my heart and soul to it when she offered it to me.'

'You were actually offered the part? You have a contract?'

'A verbal one. Which turned out not to be worth the paper it was written on, as the saying goes.'

'So what happened?' Heap said.

'Her weaselly excuse was that the producers felt I was too intense and that made me uncomfortable to watch.'

Gilchrist tried not to shake her head in bemusement. *A woman who cuts out the heart of her faithless lover too intense – surely not?*

As if to confirm it, Steadman's voice rose. '*Me*, fucking intense? What about fucking Elvira Kobel who used intensity to hide the fact she couldn't fucking act?'

Gilchrist held her breath. Heap said: 'You mean Elvira Wright, don't you?'

'The fucking Albanian bitch's name was Elvira Kobel.'

Gilchrist and Heap exchanged glances again at the name. Kobel. *Congruence*, Gilchrist mouthed. Heap raised his eyes and gave the tiniest of nods.

'How do you know that was her real name?' Heap said. 'You saw her passport?'

'I *have* her passport. And her mobile phone and laptop and all the trinkets the rich little daddy's girl got from her adoring father.'

'Rich little daddy's girl?' Heap said. 'But she lived in a squat.'

'Yeah, right. Did it look lived in to you?'

'Go on,' Gilchrist said, kicking herself for not seeing the obvious back at the squat.

'She lived in an expensive flat Daddy rented for her in Shoreditch, but she wanted the street cred of a squat too. Shoreditch is where she met Cat, in some fashionable coffee house made out of shipping containers, cardboard and recycled plastic. Cat loved all that. Loved Shoreditch. Said she wished she'd been born a man so she could grow a hipster beard like all the guys there.'

'So she got the part over you because she was Cat Pinter's new lover.'

Steadman slammed her palms down on the table. 'No! That came after. Jesus, it's like dealing with Dumb and Dumber here. Cat's producers were having trouble raising the money for this show even to happen. Then Cat met me one day, all excited, because she said a chance meeting in a café had bagged her a big investor.'

'Kobel.'

'Yes but it wasn't him she'd met.' She shook her head. 'It didn't take me long to figure out the chance meeting was with Elvira and the condition for her father, Mr Kobel, giving the money to the production was that his darling daughter got *my* part. Her rich father was the main investor in the show. Haven't you done *any* background research?'

Obviously not enough, Gilchrist thought. How did they miss that? In her case, ignorance of the way the theatre worked. 'Thank you for that background information. I'm guessing you have the address.'

It was a loft in a converted warehouse, naturally.

'Thank you for that too,' Gilchrist said. 'Would you now talk us through the crime itself, please?'

'Which one?'

'You're right,' Gilchrist said. 'Let's start with Elvira.'

'Simple enough. The obsessive little bitch spent the entire interval standing behind the curtain in her exact spot with that fucking Zimmer frame. The hardest bit was lugging the weight up the ladder to the gantry – they are bloody heavy. I took it up in the afternoon when nobody was around. It took me about twenty minutes because I had to keep stopping for a rest, wedging it in the ladder.' She laughed. Quite a pleasant laugh in the circumstances, which made it more chilling. 'I kept thinking of Sisyphus.'

'Except you accomplished your goal,' Heap said, saving Gilchrist the need to reveal she had no clue who Sisyphus was.

'That's true,' Steadman said. 'But I got quite a sweat on that afternoon, I can tell you.'

'I'm sure,' Gilchrist murmured.

'I tied it to the iron railing and came back down and waited for the evening and for her to get in place. Nobody noticed me going back up – why would they? They were all focused on their jobs. And they were all focused on what had just happened to Elvira when I came back down. So I joined everyone else hovering near her and made bleating sounds of distress.' She grinned again. 'Hilarious, really.'

Gilchrist left a pause. Heap filled it.

'And Cat Pinter?' he said. 'How did you lure her into the wood?'

'Oh, that wasn't me.' For the first time in the interview she looked at them. 'What, you think I killed her? *I* didn't kill her. I loved her!'

'How did we miss the link with Kobel?' Gilchrist said, after she'd called Sylvia Wade to get a SOCO squad from the Metropolitan Police round to the loft in Shoreditch. She wasn't expecting to find anything pertinent to Elvira's murder but perhaps there would be some indication of where Elvira's father was.

'We weren't looking for it, ma'am. No reason to.' Heap shook his head and smiled. 'Congruence or no congruence.'

They had come out of the interview room shortly after Flick's claim that she hadn't killed Cat Pinter. They were drinking surprisingly good coffee from a percolator the chief constable had installed outside the interview rooms. One of a number of percolators throughout the building because, in the chief constable's words, 'nothing is too good for my officers'.

'Call Sylvia again. Get her to source a search warrant pronto for Plumpton House so we can see if Kobel really has gone away.'

'Ma'am.' Heap phoned Wade and relayed the message. He turned to Gilchrist. 'Liesl Rabbitt's remark that Kobel had gone because he had a family tragedy to deal with has more resonance now, of course.'

'Of course. And the three decorators Sasha saw with paint on their overalls become people of interest too. We need to see if we can track them on CCTV. Let's get back in there. How do you think we should play this?'

'I think you're doing pretty well just listening, ma'am.'

Flick Steadman was chewing a nail when they walked back into the interview room. Gilchrist sat opposite her and Heap took up a position against the wall behind Steadman this time. Gilchrist turned on the recording machine again.

'If you didn't lure Cat Pinter to the wood and kill her, the obvious question I must ask is how did you end up with her heart in your bag?'

In Grahame's dressing room, Heap had signalled to Gilchrist he thought there was something in the bag. Ever the gentleman he had insisted that he would look inside the bag. The heart was at the bottom, zipped inside a freezer bag, though it wasn't frozen. Far from it.

Flick spat out a rind of nail onto the table, then examined her finger for a moment. Seemingly satisfied, she tilted her head and frowned. 'Why was it in my bag? I would have thought that was obvious. When we fell in love, we swore we would protect each other's hearts. I keep my promises. I was going to keep it with me forever.' She shrugged. 'I guess you could call me a romantic.'

That's not the first word that comes to mind, Gilchrist thought. 'Let me clarify: if you didn't kill her, who did and how did you get her heart?'

'The people I was following killed her, of course.'

'The people you were following,' Gilchrist said slowly. 'Who were you following, Ms Steadman?'

'Associates of Kobel and maybe Kobel himself, I assume.'

Gilchrist frowned. 'You know Kobel?'

'Never met the man. That's why I don't know if I was following him, Dumbo.'

'Why would it be Kobel and associates?' Gilchrist said patiently.

Steadman gazed at her, unblinking, for a minute or so. 'Clearly you know him, Detective Inspector,' she said finally. 'That's interesting.'

'He is a person of interest, but that's by the by. Why do you think he's involved?'

Steadman kind of preened. 'OK, look. When I killed Elvira – and I can't begin to tell you how satisfying it was to see that weight splatter her brains all over the curtain. It was almost better than an orgasm.' She gave a kind of shiver, then smiled flirtatiously. 'Almost.'

'Go on,' Gilchrist said, masking her distaste. 'When you killed her . . .'

'As everyone was gathered round Elvira and I'd fussed a bit, I slipped back to the dressing rooms and gathered everything of hers I could find and put them in my rucksack, which I put in the dumpster at the back of the theatre. Then when your coppers had taken my statement, I collected it and went back to my digs.

'Elvira was too stupid to have put a password in her computer, though she had on her phone. On her computer, I found her father's phone number as it was linked to her phone – cloud sharing is a great thing. It was under the listing *Daddy*.' Steadman put her finger in her open mouth and mimed retching. 'Yeck. *Daddy*. A grown woman.'

'Go on.'

'Anyway, I phoned him from a callbox round the corner – yes, there are still some that work as phones and not just places for dossers to piss in – and said his daughter had been murdered by her lesbian lover, Cat Pinter.'

She smirked. 'I'm not sure which enraged him the most – that she'd been murdered or that she was a lesbian. Macho Eastern European men, eh? *Way* behind the zeitgeist. Anyway, I gave him Cat's address in Hove – she'd been staying in an

Airbnb, but I assume you knew that. She hated it there, because it was full of moths and the place stank of all these camphor balls scattered around the place to control them.'

Well, Gilchrist didn't know any of that but she nodded anyway. The moths explained the little mystery of the camphor balls though. 'Can you give us this address?'

'Sure but I'm mid-flow here. May I finish my story first?'

'Of course,' Gilchrist said.

'So then I waited in my car in the street outside to see what would happen. They were there pretty much all night. Fortunately, I'd bought a flask and some sandwiches and I quite like middle-of-the-night radio – I alternated between some hip-hop station and talk radio – God, there are some weirdos out there in the middle of the night, aren't there?'

'There certainly are,' Gilchrist said flatly. 'What happened then?'

'Round about dawn they came out with a bundle wrapped in a rug or something – it was quite like watching an old gangster movie. So I *tailed* their car, as Humphrey Bogart or some film noir detective would do. There was more traffic than I expected at that time in the morning. That worked in my favour.'

'These men were all in overalls?' Heap said.

'That's right – dressed for the job I suppose. It wasn't so good when we came out on the A23 but I hung back – frankly with my car's pathetic horsepower I had little choice. They came off at Pyecombe, at the Hassocks–Hurstpierpoint turnoff.' She shrugged. 'And they took her to this wood.'

'You followed them into the wood?'

'Do you think I'm insane?' Gilchrist tried not to change expression. 'Of course I didn't. I waited until they'd come out and driven off then I went into the wood. I didn't really know if I'd find Cat, although I thought I'd at least find where they'd buried her. Except they hadn't buried her. She just lay there in full view. Some kind of message, I suppose – who understands the reptilian workings of the macho male mind?'

'She was dead, though?' Heap said.

'Of course she was dead!' She shook her head sorrowfully but it looked fake. 'She was bashed and battered something terrible. You wouldn't know it was her from what was left of her face.' She suddenly sobbed. 'That face I'd cupped so tenderly so many times.'

'And then you removed her heart,' Gilchrist said.

'Well, I had a good giggle first because her mouth was open. It looked like her teeth had been bashed out but I could see her mouth had been stuffed with something. It was one of those camphor balls she used to complain about. That was such a giggle.'

'And cutting the heart out?' Heap said.

'I told you. She told me she loved me with all her heart. I just wanted to see if that was true.'

'And was it?' Heap said.

Steadman beamed. 'It was!'

Gilchrist thought it best just to go with the flow, insane though the flow was. 'How did you remove it?'

'When I was a kid, I used to read Patricia Cornwell novels. Totally inappropriate, but all of my childhood was inappropriate. My father stole my childhood. He raped me on a daily basis from when I was six or so and went really crazy over me once my breasts started to grow.' She tilted her head. 'Sexual abuse was one of the things Cat and I had in common.'

'Her father raped her?' Heap said.

'Regularly. He also used to make his wife wear baby-doll nighties and teeth braces so he could pretend she was a kid too. Probably still does. Have you met them? I expect you must have.'

'The Patricia Cornwell novels?' Heap reminded her.

'Remember all those autopsies that she describes in great detail? I reckon I could have performed one myself by the age of twelve. Of course, I didn't have a Stryker saw back then to get through the breast bone.'

'Did you have one in Butcher's Wood?' Gilchrist said.

'No! Do you know how expensive they are? But I didn't need one. They'd spent all night torturing Cat and it looked like they had broken pretty much every bone in her body. I guess she wouldn't admit she'd killed the poor little rich girl – understandably, since she hadn't – or maybe they just didn't like the fact she was a lezza.

'Anyway, her chest was caved in. I'd brought a kitchen knife with me and it didn't take much to get access so I could take her heart.' She gave them a weird smile. 'And that's all she wrote.' She looked around the room as if seeing it for the first time. 'Can I have her heart back now? I'd like to go.'

Gilchrist and Heap just looked at her.

Gilchrist phoned Sylvia Wade the minute she left the interview room and gave her the Airbnb address. 'Get SOCO over there to see what they can find – which might include broken teeth.'

'Ma'am.'

'Anything at Plumpton Manor?'

'No sign of Kobel, ma'am. Mrs Rabbitt insists he went off days ago.'

'His stuff?'

'No sign of him at all, ma'am. Everything cleared out.'

'And nothing from Shoreditch?'

'A bit too early for that, ma'am.'

'True. OK, thanks. For what it's worth put out a trace on him. Contact Europol while we still can. I assume he'll be safely ensconced back in Albania by now.'

'Yes, ma'am. But there is one bit of good news.'

'Well, I'm all ears for that.'

'We found what looks like the rest of the Hassocks Blockade money in an outbuilding at Plumpton House.'

Gilchrist smiled, not that Wade would be able to see it. 'Really? That will please DS Heap.'

'Indeed, ma'am. We asked Mrs Rabbitt what she knew about it and all she said was: "Is there a reward?"'

'No surprise there,' Gilchrist said.

'She also looked pretty peeved she didn't know there was a huge stash of money on the property. And insisted she must have a right to it as that was where it was found.'

'She would.' Gilchrist shook her head – not that Wade could see that either. 'So Richard Rabbitt did find it after all. Well, well. I'll pass on the good news to DS Heap.'

TWENTY

A few days later, Heap, Bilson and Gilchrist gathered in the Cricketers again but this time with the addition of Sylvia Wade. They sat at the same table in the covered courtyard as last time.

'Job well done, you three,' Bilson said. 'Or should I say jobs plural?'

'Hardly,' Gilchrist said. 'Cat Pinter's murderers have got away and we'll probably never catch them.'

'But from what you tell me Kobel getting out of the country has slowed down the county lines drug situation round here.'

'For the time being,' Heap said.

'And Cat's father has been arrested for historic sexual abuse of her.'

'But that's not going to go anywhere, because who is there to give evidence against him?' Gilchrist said.

Bilson snorted. 'Jesus, what a pair of glass half-empty coppers they're turning out to be tonight, aren't they, Sylvia?'

'I couldn't possibly comment, sir – without another drink. I believe it's your round?'

Bilson laughed. 'I can see I'm going to have to watch you.'

While he was away from the table, Wade said: 'He's right you know, ma'am. You got some good results.'

'Sylvia is right,' Heap said. 'Even though we can't charge Clive Pyne with stabbing Darren Jones or running drugs, we've made a useful contact there to be used later.'

'And we got the money back from the Hassocks Blockade robberies,' Wade said. She saw Gilchrist's look. 'Though I don't think you're as excited about that as perhaps DS Heap is.'

'And you got the murderer of Elvira Wright locked away in a secure place,' a deep voice said. They both looked up.

'Bob Watts, as I live and breathe!' Gilchrist said. 'What are you doing here?'

'This is my mate's regular you know, Sarah, even if he's not here. I came in for a drink on Jimmy's behalf, while he's away fighting the good fight.' He indicated the glasses in his hand. 'Frank saw me at the bar and employed me as his pot-man.' He handed Gilchrist and Heap their drinks and sat down opposite them. 'May I?'

'Of course,' Gilchrist said, as Bilson came and sat beside him, handing him his pint. 'How are you?'

'I'm well and you should be pleased with yourself, because there are several jobs well done. But I'm glad I bumped into you here.' He raised his glass. 'But first: to jobs well done.'

They all raised their glasses and murmured the same thing.

'Which is a cue for you to tell us about your new job,' Bilson said.

'That's the reason I'm pleased to have bumped into you,' Watts said. He leaned forward. 'I think you all think my job as police commissioner is a Mickey Mouse job. I certainly do. So when a recruiter came along a short time ago, she caught me in a suggestible frame of mind.'

'I think within the limits of your job you've made a difference, Bob,' Heap said.

'Thanks, Bellamy, but I know I can do a lot more. And so I've taken up the offer of a job with the National Crime Agency.'

'In London?' Gilchrist said, earning an amused look from Bilson.

'Of course,' Watts said. 'But you're not getting rid of me in Brighton.'

'You're going to commute?' Heap said. 'That'll be a pain, won't it?'

'It would so, no, I don't think that will be practicable given some of the hours I'll end up working. I'm going to rent a shoebox somewhere central in London and try to make it four days up there and three days down here. But there's a lot of work to be done, so I don't quite know how that will pan out.'

'About time you got back into gear,' Bilson said, slapping Watts on his back.

'Don't I know it,' Watts said ruefully. 'What about the rest of you?'

'Same old, same old, for us, Bob,' Gilchrist said, trying not to look at him all the time. Or think about him being up in

London four days a week near to that Margaret Lively she and Bellamy had seen him with.

'I'm going up for my sergeant's exams,' Wade blurted. She looked at Gilchrist. 'With your permission, ma'am,' she said, then gulped her drink.

'Permission granted,' Gilchrist said, putting her hand on her shoulder. 'About bloody time too.' She looked at Heap. 'Competition for you, Bellamy – you'd better up your game.'

'Don't I know it,' Heap said, tilting his beer glass at Wade. 'Good luck to you.' The others raised their glasses and said the same.

Heap turned to Bilson. 'I was interested in your interest in Dante's Tuscan Italian, Mr Bilson – you know, when you quoted that bit of his poem about eating the heart.'

'Well, Bellamy, I know you'll know that until Dante came along, Italian was split between different dialects used to talk and a more formal Latin-based version for writing. He wrote in Tuscan dialect – he came from Tuscany. And it transformed Italian literature.'

'Indeed. So you're a student of Dante?'

Bilson looked around the table. 'My wife and I – ex-wife now, very sadly – bought a farmhouse in Tuscany not far from Siena after it had become Chiantishire for the English. She wanted to do cooking classes and I was to make the vineyard and the olive groves work. Well, in the course of that I became pretty fluent in Italian – I've always had an aptitude for languages.'

'And the vineyard?' Watts said.

'Doing well, I hear,' Bilson said heartily. He took a swig of his drink. 'I sold it.' He shrugged. 'Sadly the vineyard lasted longer than the marriage.' He gave a so-it-goes smile. 'Which is how I ended up in Brighton getting you lot out of scrapes with my scientific acumen.'

Watts slapped him on the shoulder. 'Your wife's loss is our gain, Frank,' he said. He raised his glass. 'Here's to scientific acumen.'

TWENTY-ONE

'**M**s Grace, how are you?'

'That depends on what blood-curdling threats you're going to make to me, Mr Goody.' Nimue Grace was curled up on the sofa in front of her log-fire, drinking a large glass of red Rioja. The phone was crooked between her shoulder and her ear.

Goody chuckled. 'No threat. I understand that the remainder of my money has been recovered by chance at Richard Rabbitt's house. Well, as best as the police can tell it's the remainder.' He chuckled again. 'Of course, if a wodge of money has gone missing they're not going to know that . . . are they?'

'I wouldn't know.'

'No, I don't suppose you would.' She heard him swallow. 'I think it would be well worth getting to know you, Ms Grace.'

'Isn't that what Hannibal Lecter says to Clarice Starling in *Silence of the Lambs*?' Grace said.

He laughed again. 'Oh I don't want to eat you, Ms Grace – delectable as you are. I think the world is a much more interesting place with you in it.'

'*That* is definitely *Silence of the Lambs*,' Grace said.

'Indeed. You know, in prison I've learned to be what people erroneously call philosophical. In fact, it's just a branch of philosophy called stoicism which has you accept what happens to you with as good a grace as you can if you can't change it.'

'Sounds wise.'

'It helps me get by.' Grace heard him sigh. 'And, you know, if someone takes a little bit of commission off the top of the discovery of the dosh, well, good luck to them I say.'

'You do?'

'I do. I hope I'll get to meet you when I get out.'

'Oh, I don't know where I'll be. The actor's life you know.'

'I thought you were retired.'

'Semi. I've been offered a Netflix series abroad. It would be my first telly, but if Meryl and Nicole can do it . . . besides I need the money.'

Goody was silent for a moment. 'Of course you do,' he finally said with a soft chuckle. Then the line went dead.

Grace went out into the garden. She had a mix of feelings. Making that horrifying discovery in the woods had really shaken her, bringing up all kinds of old, bad feelings. But her money worries were, perhaps, over. Goody's estimate was under by about a million.

When she'd gone up to London to see her agent she'd taken with her a heavy rucksack full of out-of-date money, mostly £50 notes. When Bellamy Heap had told her there was no way to trace the money and the bank wouldn't necessarily alert the police about such a deposit, it had been the green light for her.

However, she'd baulked at cashing in the whole amount. She liked to think it was because it would be greedy and wrong but that she should take some as a kind of finder's fee. But, really, if she was honest, she didn't try to cash it all because she was afraid that, despite what Heap had said, she might be found out.

She'd driven to the station via Plumpton House. She'd visited there often under the ownership prior to Richard Rabbitt's. She knew there were several outhouses that were never used and where she could park unseen from the house. If she was seen, she would claim that she was there to see about misdirected mail.

She'd lugged the bulk of the money in bin bags down into the cellar of one of the outbuildings. Nobody came to challenge her. She drove to Plumpton station, parked the car and went up to London, clasping the rucksack to her chest.

In London, she went to the Bank of England first. It was imposing but it had a counter service like any other. However, she went to the information desk and explained she had rather a lot of out-of-date money she wanted to convert. He ushered her into a wood-panelled side room and a middle-aged man in a three-piece pinstripe suit bustled in, shook her hand, eyed the bag and lifted it onto the table in the centre of the room.

'May I?' he said as he lifted the top flap of the rucksack.

'Of course.'

He peered inside and rummaged his hand as far as he could get it. He nodded to himself and pressed a bell on the table. A younger man came in and the older man gestured to the rucksack. 'Count this please, Crispin.'

The young man picked the rucksack up and left the room. Grace watched it go. The older man caught something in the expression on her face. 'Never fear, madam,' he said with an avuncular smile. 'This is the Bank of England. We won't steal a penny.'

She smiled and looked at him questioningly. He smiled back. 'In your case this is just a formality. You prove your identity – I assume you have a passport with you? Good. And then you give us your bank details and once the money is counted we pay the conversion amount into your account. Assuming all those bills are of more or less the same denomination that will probably be somewhere near the three million mark. You will receive that in due course.'

'And that's all?'

'Ordinarily there are some checks and procedures to follow.' He gave his avuncular smile. 'But I'm not sure they're necessary in your case, Ms Grace.'

'You keep saying in my case . . .'

'Well, I don't see the need to give someone as successful as you the third degree to find out where you got the money – it's obvious where you got it. And if you chose to keep your money under your mattress or wherever you have kept it, that's your business. You'll be surprised how many people do keep money under the mattress, by the way.'

'You know who I am?' Grace said, her heart sinking. So much for anonymity. Oh well, in for a penny. She gave him The Smile. 'I'm flattered.'

'No, madam – I'm honoured. Of course I know who you are. Although I'm not a film-goer, I'm an avid theatre person. Your comic timing in the various Tom Stoppard and Oscar Wilde plays I have been privileged to see you in has been superb and enhanced each play.'

Grace affected false modesty. Well, she had been bloody good in them but she couldn't admit that, could she? 'With writers

as talented as those two, you can't go wrong, as long as you
don't, as the saying goes, bump into the furniture – and, in fact,
in comedies you can get away with that too.' She gave him a
tinkling laugh for good measure.

They made more theatre talk until Crispin came back in with
various papers. Grace got out her passport. Ten minutes later,
she walked out of there to a taxi rank and bound up the stairs
to her agent when she alighted in front of her office in Brewer
Street in the centre of Soho.

She came out of there even more elated. Her agent had
ambushed her with a producer for a Netflix series, but in her
happiness Grace was clearly exuding That Thing that made
some actors movie stars because audiences can't look away
from them. She was offered the lead on the spot. And, frankly
even more exciting for Grace, was a request from *Desert Island
Discs* to go on the show.

She'd been asked to do it almost at the start of her career
but had thought they were daft to ask her too early so had said
a snooty No. Now that her career had tanked, she'd never
expected to be offered it again.

On the train down to Hassocks, she was figuring out
which music tracks to choose for her desert island. She was
still vaguely thinking about that when she entered Butcher's
Wood . . .

EPILOGUE

Heap sat in his garden with a mug of coffee looking at the blank wall of Lewes prison a couple of hundred yards across the scrubland on the other side of the garden. Graham Goody, the Hassocks Blockade robber – though never convicted of the crime, of course – was behind that wall somewhere. He would have heard by now the money had been recovered and placed in the public purse.

Heap thought about the happy circumstance that led to the recovery. Kobel, the ostensible object of the search of Plumpton House, was long gone. The discovery of the money was an unexpected bonus.

The assumption was that Rabbitt had found it in white containers at Grace's lake just a couple of days before he died. He'd had just enough time to transfer it to black bags but not enough time to do anything with it before he was murdered at Grace's lake.

Perhaps one of the reasons he'd been down at the lake the day he was killed was to see if there was any more money in other containers.

Heap took a sip of his coffee and looked at the papers spread before him at his breakfast table. It was his family history project. He rubbed his eyes. Perhaps he'd leave it for a bit.

He was feeling sorry for himself because he didn't think Kate was ever coming back to him. He sighed. Aside from anything else, he wished he'd known that the last time they'd made love would actually be the last time.

He picked up the *Guardian* and scanned the headlines in a desultory way. No news that particularly interested him. The President of the United States of America was continuing to be a petulant buffoon, so no change there. The UK government claimed the economy was on track for a boom despite all evidence to the contrary so same old, same old there.

There was a sidebar about an outbreak of some new virus

on the other side of the world in a Chinese province called
Wuhan. The authorities had notified the World Health
Organization, as any country was formally obliged to do, and
put Wuhan under lockdown to ensure the virus remained local-
ized and didn't spread into other regions of China.

And that was about it. He turned to the crossword.

PILLGWENLLY